THE
NEW-CUT
ROAD

THE
NEW-CUT
ROAD

by Naomi Talley

HAWTHORN BOOKS, INC.
Publishers
New York

Designed by Martin J. Baumann

*This book is for
Susan and Marc.*

THE
NEW-CUT
ROAD

Chapter 1

I *had turned seventeen before Mama would admit that* our town, Lynwood, in the Indian Territory, was a fit and proper place to rear a daughter. By that time I was leaving to teach a rural school, and the Indian Territory, together with the Oklahoma Territory, was about to become the new state of Oklahoma.

As Papa's bride, Mama had come from Georgia with dire forebodings to make a home in the Indian Territory. The Indian raids and bandits she had worried about had not materialized, but when I came along that first year, Papa said I made a perfect substitute. My blood-curdling yells in the middle of the night could rival those of any raiding party. Mama could worry about my teething, colds, and colic, and an endless assortment of worries lay ahead.

From the time I lost my front teeth, Mama had worried about my matrimonial prospects. That was when she decided my straight hair would be permanently rust-colored and not the dusky, curling ringlets she had hoped for. I was just pure Blake from way back, Papa said, and she might as well become reconciled to it. But she hoped my hair would darken as I grew older and maybe not be so straight. Papa said his hadn't, as she could well see, but he did expect my looks to improve over the toothless phase. Mama sighed and asked how I always managed to tear all the ruffles off my petticoats. Why couldn't I be like Susybelle Lacy? Susybelle was such a little lady.

"Mag's to blame," I told her. "Mag's a mean, stubborn old horse. She walks right under the apple tree and rakes me off and the limbs catch the old ruffles and I hate ruffles and wish you'd never put another embroidery ruffle on anything and I hate Susybelle Lacy."

"I do wish you weren't such a tomboy, Prissy," Mama said. "When I was your age, I played with dolls and wore white dresses and starched, embroidered pantalets. I was afraid of horses."

Papa said he could well see how with starched pantalets she would be afraid of horses, but let the kid have her fun. "What do a few torn ruffles amount to in the long run if Priss learns to stay on a horse? There's a lot to be learned from horses, Sally. You ought to study them more."

Ever since I learned to walk I wanted a horse of my own. When I was four, Papa would put me on Mag and let me ride around the yard. Mag was a blazed-faced sorrel pony, fat as a butterball and her back flat as the floor. She was independent and stubborn as a mule. She would walk around the yard until she had had enough and then would come to a dead stop under a tree. I would whack her fat rump with my peach-tree switch and yell and kick her sides, but she would not budge. I would sit there and bawl until someone took me down, and then I would yell to get back up. Mag always had her way, but I never wanted to give up. I was determined to make her go where I wanted her to go. Papa said I would learn horse sense sooner or later. He was right. Later, much later, I realized what he meant.

When I was ten and Pinky six, Papa bought a phaeton for Mama. She just had to have one, she said. It was the first in Lynwood. The sides were so shiny we could see our faces in them. There were lamps on each side that looked like silver, but nobody ever lighted them. Pinky and I were not allowed to touch it for fear we would scratch the shining paint.

By the time I was old enough to drive the phaeton to town, the shine had worn off, and it had acquired some scratches and a few dents in the fenders. In the summertime I would drive to the post office every day after dinner for the mail. About half a mile down the street from our house I would turn west, then ahead two blocks, turn south again, and on down the hill to the post office.

I liked the Saturday trips. That was the day the postmaster gave away uncalled-for papers and magazines. With people changing addresses, sometimes suddenly and without notice, there was always an accumulation of magazines. I would go home with all I could carry. These magazines were printed on cheap wood-pulp paper, their pages filled with sentimental continued stories and advertisements for love charms and liver pills. Most of the stories were about English lords and ladies and their poor kitchen maids, who turned out to be the real daughters of the lords. Papa did not know about the story papers. I kept them out of sight when he was around.

After I turned the corner on the straight road home on these Saturday trips, I would read my continued story while Mag ambled along at a slow trot. I wanted to see what happened to Becky, the gatekeeper's daughter, who was in love with young Lord Alfred, who could not marry her because he must marry the beautiful Lady Gwendolyn, Lord Devondevon's heiress.

One day I could not wait to turn onto the straight road home before starting the final chapter of my story. Becky was deep in the gloomy forest, on a high cliff overlooking the lake. It was Lord Alfred's wedding day, and she had left him a note that she had gone away, never to return. She heard the village bells ring out. She heard galloping hoofs; she felt herself going over. . . .

I came back to earth the hard way. It was not poor Becky going over. I had gone over. Jogging along unheeded, Mag had turned the corner too short. The inside wheels climbed the slanting post that divided the sidewalk from the street, and the buggy went over flat on its side. Mag stopped and stood patiently, one shaft pushing against her fat side and the other high in the air.

It was a hot afternoon, and few people were about. I climbed out and waited for someone to come along. And who should come but Deefy Jones, the one person I hated as only a fourteen-year-old can hate. Deefy had told around that I was his girl. I had been teased so much about Deefy that I could not stand the sound of his name. He was not deaf. He was just slow in absorbing the meaning of words put together in sentences. He would stand and look at you blankly until you repeated what you had said. It was this strained, listening look that got him his name.

I tried to ignore Deefy as he drove up. I paid not the slightest attention to him as he climbed out of his delivery cart but looked away as if turning over a buggy in the street was an everyday affair not deserving of a second glance.

"Did ya have a runaway, Prissy?" he stuttered, after absorbing the situation through his open mouth.

Anything more ridiculous than Mag staging a runaway could not be imagined. I wanted to tell Deefy so but did not want him standing around with his mouth open. Lady Gwendolyn was fresh in my mind. She had just discovered

Becky in Lord Alfred's arms. "Please go, Deefy," I said coldly. "You can be of no assistance. I prefer to be alone."

Deefy's chin dropped, and his eyes crossed. He looked at me in that rapt, listening way of his, then guffawed loud and long. "Aw, now, Prissy, you're jest a-foolin', ain't ya?"

I wanted to bash his face in, but just then it seemed everybody in town was out for a drive on that street. A red-wheeled rig drove up. In it were a man and a boy, both in white linen clothes. The boy looked a little older than I, and his hair was smoothed back as if he had just come from the barber shop. He jeered at me. "Some trick, kiddo. They pay for that in Sells-Floto circus. Try them." The man handed him the reins and got out.

Two men in a farm wagon stopped and got out. Then, to cap it all, in their clean little rubber-tired surrey, pulled by a clean little white pony, came Mrs. Lacy and Susybelle, all white fresh-ironed ruffles and blue ribbons and blonde curls. I loathed Susybelle. She was always so clean and her curls in perfect order. She was afraid of horses and shrieked at bugs and worms when boys were around.

"My goodness, Priscilla Blake, what have you done now?" Mrs. Lacy screamed. "Are you hurt?"

Susybelle laughed. With one scornful look she had taken in my faded gingham dress, my loose hair, and my bare feet stuck in old shoes. She had also taken in the dressed-up boy in the fancy rig. "Of course she's not hurt, Mama. She did it on purpose to show off to Deefy Jones. He's stuck on her."

I had to shut my mouth and clamp my teeth down hard to keep from saying anything. While the boy held the team of dappled grays, the man found a pole nearby and helped the farmers lever the buggy back on its four wheels. "You'd better watch where you're going, sister," one of the men said, "and quit making sheep-eyes at boys while you're driving."

"So you're Priscilla Blake," the man in the white suit said. "Could you be Tom Blake's daughter?"

Very much embarrassed, I said, "Yes, sir, I am."

The big man grinned. "I should have known it—that hair and those eyes and such complete indifference to driving a horse." He handed me the reins. "Tell your father that Ham Harper sends his respects and that I'll be around to see him tomorrow. Maybe I'll bring my boy if I can drag him along. This is my son, Richard, Priscilla."

But I wouldn't look. I was so ashamed of my appearance I could not say a word. I climbed into the phaeton without more than a "thank you" and drove off. I whipped old Mag into such a trot that she was in a lather when we reached home.

I did not tell Mama about the incident, but it got to her fast. Everyone in town soon heard about it. Those whom Susybelle did not carry the news to, Deefy Jones did. Poor Mama was distressed to death. "I'll never live down the disgrace," she said mournfully. "To think Judge Hammond Harper saw you. And his son, Richard. Oh, Priscilla, I knew he was coming and had such hopes of your making an impression on him—and his son."

"I did, Mama, the worst kind."

Sunday morning I asked Mama to let me take Pinky to Aunt Emma's to spend the day. She was in such a flutter about the Judge coming she said yes. I did not go home until sundown and missed seeing Judge Hammond Harper and his duded-up son.

Chapter 2

Lynwood's big entertainment feature, guaranteed to bring out everyone in town and the surrounding countryside, was its parades. Any event, from a county election to the mayor's birthday, called for a parade.

From the time the business section of the town was two stores and a blacksmith's shop until long after Main Street had grown to be a real thoroughfare, the life of Lynwood was influenced by its parades. Boys practiced for hours on band instruments throughout the school year for the brief glory of marching on parade days. Elocution teachers had regular weekly tableaux drills to keep the girls ready for manning the floats. Rivalry was strong between church societies to see which could send out the most spectacular float. The town merchants bought regular supplies of colored gauze, cheesecloth, and calico for parade costumes and trimmings.

It was hard to see how an audience could be gathered

for the event, since everyone who had the slightest excuse
or a horse marched or rode in the parade. Yet by sunrise
on parade days all the hitching posts were taken by teams
of the more prosperous country people who could afford
the twenty-five-cent fee. Sidewalks along the parade route
were filled early, and eating places were crowded all day.
Cracker-and-cheese customers ate in the stores or on boxes
along the sidewalks. Almost everyone gathered at the picnic grounds after the parade, where dinner was spread and
speakers and band music filled the air. Sometimes there
would be a balloon ascension.

Seth Porter, who owned the town's one transfer system,
always loaned his two draywagons and teams to be used
for floats. Women worked far into the night before parades, trimming the drays with paper flowers and bunting.
Schoolgirls draped with colored cheesecloth posed in tableaux on the floats. Little girls in their best starched white
dresses marched with the small boys ahead of the floats.

The town's brass band, coached and drilled by Mrs.
Watts, the band teacher, headed the procession. Mrs.
Watts, plump and short-legged as a mallard duck, marched
ahead, tooting her trombone and stamping along in a
tight-fitting uniform from which it looked as if the brass
buttons would pop at any minute. Her boots and breeches
had been the talk of the town when she first came, but
she married Dick Watts, the druggist, organized a brass
band, and arranged parades which were such successes
that people forgot to talk about her.

The dream of my life had been to ride a prancing horse
in a parade, dressed in a costume, with flags waving and
the band playing. But Mama said no. Riding with men and
boys in a public parade was not ladylike, and she would
not even consider it. She would have been happy, of course,
to see me pose in a tableau on a float. Girls for the tableaux were chosen from Miss Elton's elocution class, so

Mama had me take elocution all one year, hoping I would be chosen for Sleeping Beauty or something. That, she felt, would establish my social standing.

The year I was fifteen Miss Elton asked me to be the witch in Hansel and Gretel. I said I would rather be the giant in Jack and the Beanstalk. I could get a pair of stilts and wear long pants over them and put on a long red beard.

Miss Elton looked very disapproving. "I must say, Priscilla, I do think you wouldn't always want to wear pants. You're almost old enough to be having beaux. Most girls your age are starting a hope chest and thinking of getting married."

"Well, I'm not," I assured her emphatically. "I'm never going to marry, Miss Elton. I'm going to be an old maid like you."

Miss Elton turned red as a beet. She stared at me, her mouth and eyes round as buttons. She swallowed hard and put her hands behind her and said something about, oh, give her strength, and hurried away. She never again asked me to be in a tableau.

Mama grieved about it, but I said flatly I would not stand up on a float in a cheesecloth nightgown with paper wings for anybody. I wanted to ride a horse.

"Oh, Priscilla," Mama said, scolding, "if you could only get horses out of your head. Don't you ever think of being a lady?"

"Do I have to?" I groaned. All the ladies I knew sat around and made embroidery or sewed lace on ruffles and then sewed the ruffles on things nobody ever saw. They laced their corsets so tight they could not walk a block without getting out of breath. When they had beaux, they were fluttery and giggled behind fans and blushed. When they married, they had babies and got fat and didn't curl their hair anymore. Except Mama. Mama wasn't fat, and

her hair was naturally curly. "I don't want to be a lady,"
I announced flatly. "Not ever."

Mama shook her head, and her brown eyes misted over.

When Pinky bolted into the room one hot August afternoon and pushed a pink handbill under my nose, I knew
something big was up. He had been running; his face was
red and perspiring, and his short hair stood straight up
in the cowlick he hated.

"Look at this, Priss; look at it. The biggest thing that
ever happened in this burg. A parade and real money
prizes for the best riders." Pinky's voice trailed from a
croak to a squeak. "Read it," he said, panting. "An all-day
parade and everything—see—"

"I see. Keep still while I read it."

There in letters four inches high on the bright pink
paper was the big news:

Labor Day Celebration

All-Day Picnic ❋ ❋ ❋ Free Barbecue

Mammoth Parade

Floats ❋ Costumed Riders ❋ Bands

$25 Prizes $25

For Best Man and Woman Riders

Political Speaking—Greased-Pig Race

Square Dances—Fiddlers' Contest

Balloon Ascension—Fireworks

Pinky's eyes were shining. "Priss, I just gotta ride in
that parade. I can go as a wild Indian. I just gotta ride."

I shook my head. "Pinky, people would think, the way
you talk, that you had lived in the backwoods all your life.
Honestly, haven't you ever looked inside a grammar?"

"Aw, you know what I mean, Sis. I don't have to talk
grammar to you." He grinned and wriggled his ears, and I

had to laugh. "Priss, think of it. Twenty-five dollars. Maybe I could win that. You know I can ride good."

"Sure, I know you can ride, but Mama wouldn't let you, and you know it," I said. I wanted to ride too and knew how he felt.

"Heck, I never get to do anything," Pinky grumbled as he stalked off.

Chapter 3

*T*he more I thought about the parade, the more I wanted to ride in it. Mama had been talking about sending me away to school in another year. At seventeen she thought I should have a little polishing off. Papa said I was all right. I was smart enough in my books, and I'd settle down and wear frills one of these days. But Mama had Georgia in mind, and I knew that if I did not ride in the parade this time, I might never have another chance. Once I got to Georgia, they would tie me up in starched pantalets and hoops—I supposed they still wore them there—and they would make a lady out of me in spite of everything.

The year Mag died, Pinky and I had discovered Dr. Rutherford's horses in a pasture across the railroad tracks. They were easy to catch if we fed them shelled oats. They would run to meet us when they saw us coming. We would slip a rope through the halter rings and ride around the pasture like wild Indians.

One day when we had been running the horses full tilt, old Doc Rutherford drove up. Pinky and I had never asked permission to ride the horses, and we were scared stiff. Doc opened the gate and came inside.

"I see you're giving my horses a workout," he said brusquely. "They need it. No one ever rides them anymore since the children left home."

"Do you mind?" I asked. "We don't always run them like this, but they like to run."

My face must have been pretty long, for the doctor laughed.

"Of course they like to run. They're running stock, trained for the track. That chestnut you're riding, Priscilla, carried off many a purse in years gone by. Scheherazade, she is. My daughter called her Zade. The bay there is Rumido. He had all the makings of a fine racer until he pulled a tendon and I took him out of track running. Go ahead, kids, ride them whenever you want to. It's good for them."

When the doctor got into his buggy to leave, he called to us, "Come over and get their saddles and bridles any time. They're in the barn, and Jed will get them for you."

We never went for the saddles. We were afraid Mama would find out and stop us from riding. I told Papa about it, and he said he guessed it was all right for us to ride, but he did think I'd better find a pair of his pants to ride in. After all, I was getting to be a big girl.

Pinky and I had been riding Doc Rutherford's horses in the pasture one afternoon and were walking home. "Pinky, I want to ride in that parade, too," I said. "I'll never get over it if I don't. We're going to ride, Pinky, and I am going to win that prize money. I'll put it away to buy a horse when I can save enough."

"Sure we'll ride, Priss. We're going to fly to the moon,

too, just like this." Pinky waved his arms and puffed out his cheeks, exploding his breath noisily.

"All right, smarty, if you're not interested," I said.

"Okay, spill the beans." Pinky could be very patronizing at times.

I walked ahead, whistling, but Pinky caught up with me and poked me in the ribs. "Go on, tell it," he squeaked.

"Tell you how we'll fly to the moon? I've not figured it out yet."

"Okay, I'm sorry. Now tell me how we are going to ride in the parade when we don't even have any horses."

"We'll ride Zade and Rummy. I'll ask Doc if we can have them."

Pinky grunted. "Mama won't let you ride, and you know it. And Doc won't let anyone ride his horses in a parade, and you know that."

"Of course Mama wouldn't let me ride, but she must not know. And she won't know if you don't tell her. Cross your heart you will not tell her, and hope to die if you do, and I will ask Doc for his horses."

Pinky wanted to ride as much as I did. Mama would let him ride if he had a gentle horse, but I knew she would never allow me to do it if she knew. Mama enjoyed a parade as much as anyone, but for her daughter to ride was out of the question.

Mrs. Watts, the bandleader, assigned places and costumes if she approved of the applicants, and she was a strict judge. "There'll be no carryings-on in my parades," she had said. I knew before I asked Doc for his horses, I had better see Mrs. Watts. As soon as Pinky and I got home, I changed to a dress and went to the Watts Music Studio, which was what Mrs. Watts called her house.

She was giving Bunk Edwards a lesson. Bunk had worked and sweated every summer for three years, trying to learn to play the slide trombone. The unearthly sounds he brought forth from the instrument were enough to discourage anyone else, but not Bunk. They only stimulated him to further effort, for as soon as he could play "America," he could be in the band, and Bunk was determined to march with the band come parade days.

I stuck my fingers in my ears to shut out the screeching. Mrs. Watts took the trombone, showed Bunk how to place his fingers, and played a few notes. Bunk pursed his lips and blew. It sounded like our tomcat when the cow stepped on his tail at milking time.

"That will do for this time, Bunk," Mrs. Watts said. She dropped into a rocking chair and fanned her pink face with a palm-leaf fan. The afternoon was hot and still, and her brassy, blonde hair hung in limp, straight wisps instead of the frizzy curls she usually wore.

"Well?" She tucked up her wispy hair. "What is it you want, Priscilla? This is my lesson day, you know."

"I came on business," I said. "I'd like to . . ."

"Oh, you want to learn to play in the band? That is good. I want girls in my band, but they won't come. Their mothers say no, it is not ladylike, so girls must not play in the band. Pish, posh!"

When Mrs. Watts stopped for breath, I was ready. "May I ride in the parade, Mrs. Watts? I can ride a horse."

She stopped rocking. "You ride in the parade, Priscilla? Whatever would you ride?"

"I have a horse, Mrs. Watts. I mean, I'll get a horse. Pinky and I want to ride."

"Oh, I see. So you'll ride Doc Rutherford's horses. Yes, I know you can ride. I've seen you in the pasture. But would your mother let you ride?"

"She wouldn't if she knew. But I thought we could work out some sort of costume so she would not mind afterwards. We'd let it be a surprise."

"Oh, oh, I have the very thing." Mrs. Watts jumped up and ran back to her bedroom. In a few minutes she was back with a dusty box, which she plumped down on a chair and untied. Proudly she shook out a pair of long, thin-legged red-flannel pants and a short coat.

"This you can wear," she said. "I myself wore it when I was your size." She held up the pants against her plump middle. "I was a devil then—in a play," she added hastily. "Such a nice play. Oh dear, why did I ever get so fat like this? I was such a thin one."

She handed the pants to me. "Put them on, Priscilla," she ordered. "There is a tail, a nice long one." She fumbled in the box. "You can be a devil, too," she said, panting, "in the parade. The tail will stand straight up behind you on the horse. It is wired—the tail. Oh, why didn't I think of it before? Never have I had a devil in a parade."

I held up the thin-legged red pants and the long-sleeved, thin red coat. It would be like wearing a red-flannel union suit, a union suit with a wired tail that would stand up straight behind me. It would be bad enough if Mama ever found I rode in the parade wearing my Sunday best, but to ride as a devil, a red one with a long tail standing up behind me on the horse—it would never do.

Mrs. Watts found the tail and waved it before me. Such a tail. Even the forked end of it was there. "Isn't it lovely?" she shrieked. "A devil, a red devil, will be perfect for you, Priscilla."

The thought of those red-flannel pants on a hot day started me itching. And the thought of Mama, if I wore them, made me even more uncomfortable. I was miserable. If I said no, Mrs. Watts probably would not let me ride at all, and if I wore that outfit, we'd just have to bury Mama. I could not do it.

"I can't wear it, Mrs. Watts. If you knew Mama . . . "

"I do know your mama," she said. "She is a good woman

but so old-fashioned. For her, a girl should still wear hoops.
Oh, these perfect ladies," she moaned. "They make my life
so hard." She shook her head. Perspiration dripped from
her nose, and she wiped her face with the red-flannel pants.

"So you want to ride, but you won't be a devil. You'd
make such a good one, Priscilla," she said wistfully as she
folded the flannel devil's-suit and threw it back into the
box. "Get your own costume and let me know what it will
be. Pinky can be a cowboy." She shook her finger sternly.
"I want no more Indians, mind you. I'm sick of Indians.
Why do all the boys want to be Indians? They even come
from out of town wanting to stick a feather in their hair
and paint their faces. Not a turkey in the country has a
decent tailfeather left."

I went home and told Pinky that he could ride and go as
a cowboy. I was sure Doc would let us ride Zade and
Rummy. Pinky had a dingy white-felt hat Uncle John had
given him. It would be easy to borrow a bright-colored shirt
for him, but getting a costume for myself would not be so
easy. After supper I told Pinky I was going to see Doc.

"I'm coming along, too," Pinky said. "I want to see the
saddles."

"No, Pinky, you can see the saddles later if we ride. You
stay home."

Pinky grumbled. He felt abused, but he often felt that
way, and I was not too sorry for him.

Chapter 4

It was a fine August evening with a pleasant breeze from the south. Doc was sitting on his front veranda. The yard was a solid mass of petunias and four-o'clocks.

I sat down on the steps and leaned back against a pillar. "You have such a nice place here, Doc. It's so peaceful and quiet. And such a nice view of the Washita Valley."

"Yes, it's a nice place, but I've got no one to enjoy it with me anymore. No wife, no children—just a doddering old man left with his memories."

"Oh, ho," I jeered. "You, doddering? Not if what I hear about you is true. What about your threatening to horsewhip that drunk Hoot Bender last week? Who won that match?"

The doctor chuckled. "Now, Priss, don't tell me you heard about that little episode. It didn't amount to a thing. Not a thing. Hoot could have broken me clean in two, and he knew it."

"Yes, maybe, but he didn't. You backed him all the way off the sidewalk and into the muddy street."

"Well, he'll learn to keep his low remarks to himself when there are ladies passing," Doc said hotly. "If he'd been where I lived in Kentucky, he would have got a horsewhipping and a feather party to boot."

"All right, but how about your taking Rummy out and racing that Bar-X cowboy on a fifty-dollar bet until he had to eat your dust. Who won that bet?"

Doc whooped. "Prissy, you should have seen that one. That was really good. That crowd thought they'd have to send for the undertaker when they saw me get on that horse."

"Gosh, Doc, I just have to ride in the parade. I came to ask you if Pinky and I may ride Zade and Rummy. If you will let me ride and I can get a costume, Mrs. Watts will let me be in the parade."

Doc bristled. "Oh, she will, eh? Damned decent of her. And your mother? What about her, Priss? Will she let you ride?"

"She knows I want to ride, but she says a lady would not ride in a parade."

"Well, I'll be doggoned if she wouldn't," Doc exploded. "And who says a lady would not ride in this little two-bit parade? Well, that's all she knows about it. Little does she know what a real Kentucky lady would do. If my Debbie were here, she'd ride in that parade, and my Debbie was very much a lady, a real Kentucky-bred lady." Doc looked off toward the fading sunset and hammered on the chair with his clenched fist.

"Who was Debbie?" I asked. It helped to know that someone who was very much a lady would want to ride in a parade.

"Debbie was the most beautiful girl in all Kentucky, and I married her."

Doc went into the parlor and brought out an old yellowplush album and a red-velvet miniature case. "This one was made just before we were married," he said. It was the portrait of a lovely pink-cheeked girl with big brown eyes, her dark hair caught up on top of her head with a gold-backed comb. She wore a gold locket hung from a black-velvet ribbon. Her blue dress was low on her white shoulders.

"She's lovely, Doc," I said. "Too pretty to be real. Did she really ride?"

Doc looked at the picture. "She was very real," he said. He laid the case on the table and opened the album. There was a picture of Miss Debbie in her riding habit for side-saddle. I looked at the picture a long time—at the trim, dainty figure, the proud head with the saucy derby and veil, and the long skirt caught up at the left to show a high boot.

"Why doesn't Mama want me to ride?" I asked. "Mama says women who ride and stay around horses are mannish. Miss Debbie doesn't look mannish."

"Your mother just doesn't know horses, Priscilla—or, I might say, women."

Dozie, Doc's housekeeper, came out just then with a pitcher and a plate of cookies. "Here's your lemonade, Mister Doc," she said. "It will cool you off, you and Miss Prissy."

We sat for a while drinking Dozie's lemonade and looking at the last colored streaks in the west. "Doc, I just have to ride in that parade. Next year I'll be eighteen, and I would never get to ride then." Eighteen seemed so old.

Doc lit his pipe and puffed away to get it going. "Priss, your mother would never forgive me. You know that."

"But I could dress up so no one would know me, not even Mama." Then I told him about Mrs. Watts and the devil suit. Doc laughed until Dozie came running out to see what was the matter.

"Well, you know what it will be if I help you," he said weakly. "It sounds like collusion to me."

"It's not that bad, Doc. It's not going to hurt anyone."

Doc puffed some more on his pipe, then knocked out the ashes on the porch railing. "You win, Priss. I'll do it. There was never a time when I didn't like a good joke. It will be a good one on everyone. Of course, it won't hurt anybody. Your mother has sense. She'll laugh too when it's over. You want to ride in the parade. All right, can you ride side-saddle?"

"Sidesaddle? Why, Doc, I've never been on any kind of saddle. Do I need a saddle?"

"Well," Doc said brusquely, "of course, you might paint your face, stick a feather in your hair, and go as Pocohon-tas, although it's pretty hot for a blanket."

"But Mrs. Watts doesn't want any more Indians."

Doc laughed. "Priss, you're priceless sometimes. There is just one thing to do. If you ride, you will have to ride sidesaddle. I have the very costume for you."

If I rode sidesaddle, sitting up on a pillion like Lady Guinevere or whoever she was, it would spoil the parade for me. Almost, I'd rather not ride at all.

"Doc, do I have to do that? Riding sidesaddle isn't rid-ing. I'd as soon sit in a chair strapped on the horse's back."

"But that's where you are wrong, girl. It takes a good rider to ride sidesaddle. That is the way English women ride, and you can't look down your nose at their riding. They ride sidesaddle after the hounds and jump fences and hedges. Anybody can stay on astride, or should, but it takes perfect balance and self-confidence to ride sidesaddle. That's the only reason I suggest it. I know you can ride."

"But Doc, nobody rides sidesaddle now. They just don't do it anymore."

"No, Priscilla," Doc said testily. "Nobody around here rides like wild Indians, either. I'm surprised at you. A girl who would ride in the parade without her mother's permission won't ride sidesaddle because people might laugh at her. That doesn't make sense, Priss. At least, not for you." He chuckled. "You just can't give up. You want to wear pants. That's the whole thing, isn't it?"

I had to laugh then. "I guess that's it, Doc. What's the costume?"

"The one Debbie wore in that picture. I never thought I'd let anyone else wear it, but I think Debbie would want it that way. Come over tomorrow morning, and we'll look at the saddles."

I was over bright and early the next morning. We went through the peach orchard to the barn lot. Old Jeb was working on some harness under the hay shed.

"Jeb, get Miss Debbie's saddle, and let's look it over," Doc said. "This little lady here might have a use for it."

Old Jeb straightened his crooked back. His wrinkled old face screwed up into a tight frown as he looked from Doc to me. "What do you want Miss Debbie's saddle for?" he asked scoldingly. "Miss Debbie told me she never wanted you to sell her saddle." He thought a minute. "I declare to my soul, Mister Doc, I just don't recollect where I put that saddle."

Doc laughed. "Get on in there, Jeb, and get that saddle. Nobody's going to sell it. Miss Prissy here might want to ride it in the parade. Don't you think Miss Debbie would like that?"

Old Jeb laughed shrilly. "She would that, Mister Doc; she would that." He disappeared into the barn, came back with the saddle, and set it on the harness block. He went over it carefully with a piece of clean cotton cloth, but it was easy to see there was no dust on it.

Doc held up the stirrup. It was like a twisted silver rope. "See this stirrup? I had it made for Debbie before we married. She was a fine rider. She rode Zade's grandmother in a race in Kentucky once and won the big purse. The jockey didn't show up. He turned crooked and was going to get the mare scratched, but Debbie wouldn't stand for it. She got into his clothes and twisted her curls tight under the cap and rubbed dirt on her hands and face. No one knew until the race was over that Deborah Wainwright rode the winning horse. Some folks said she'd be disgraced, but not my Debbie. She was Kentucky blueblood, same as Zade. There ought to be more women in this world like my Debbie."

Doc twirled his watch chain and looked away toward the river. The watch chain had a little silver stirrup hanging from it, just like the one on the saddle. After a moment he asked, "Do you want to ride sidesaddle, Priss?"

"Yes, sir," I said quickly. "I'd be proud to ride Miss Debbie's saddle if Jeb will teach me how."

Chapter 5

I made Pinky solemnly promise he would not tell anyone about my being in the parade. He was so excited about riding Rummy he would have promised anything. Mama was so busy getting ready for the picnic that she didn't pay any attention to Pinky and me. She had baked cakes and pies and made potato salad for the picnic dinner. There would be free barbecue and bread for everyone, but Mama would have her fried chicken. People would spread dinner with their friends and neighbors and make a regular feast.

All Pinky could talk about was his boots and Stetson and chaps. He had managed to borrow a pair of mangy-looking goatskin chaps from someone. "Keep those things away from me," I said. "They must have been the first pair Robinson Crusoe made for himself when times were so hard."

Pinky snorted. "You just don't know how important a good pair of chaps is. You just don't know anything about

25

riding. Anyone knows a cowboy riding in the brush could get himself ripped to pieces without a good pair of chaps."

To hear Pinky talk, you would have thought that chaps were more important than the horse. I told him chaps were out of place on a Kentucky thoroughbred, but he gave me to understand that all cowboys wore chaps and that no horse was too good to be a cowhorse.

On the morning of the parade we were up early. Mama was busy frying chicken and packing the food for dinner. She would not let me help, saying I would just be in the way. She wanted to get through early so she could go to the parade.

I told Mama I would be in the parade. She was packing a big white coconut cake in the basket. "Couldn't I have just one little piece of cake now?" I asked, knowing, of course, that I could not. I wanted to get her mind off the parade.

"No, of course not, Priscilla. Whose float will you ride on?" Mama bustled around, and I emptied the sugarbowl into my handkerchief to take to Zade.

"Just you look good, and you will see me. I will be in costume, and I'll bet you won't know me." I ran the tip of my finger around the edge of the plate for loose coconut. "You wouldn't give me one crumb, would you?"

"I would not cut this cake now for the governor," Mama said scoldingly. "Now run along. Oh, that reminds me. I am going to ask Governor Harper to eat with us. He is going to speak today. And do look your best, Priscilla. He has a fine-looking son, you know. Richard goes to college. He might be there. I'll never get over your running away when he came that time."

"But Judge Harper is not governor yet. He may not get elected."

"Well, I think he will be. He is a fine man, and Papa is going to vote for him. Do take pains with your dressing.

I made that blue swiss just for this picnic, and I want to be proud of you."

"I'll do my best," I promised, "but I wish Papa could be here."

"He may get in," Mama said. "He promised he'd try. But hurry home right after the parade and change. We'll have the same table we always have—under the big pecan tree by the grandstand."

I went on over to Doc's and stopped by the barn lot to see if the horses were ready. Old Jeb had curried and brushed them until their coats shone like satin. Zade came over and rubbed her nose against me. I gave her the handful of sugar.

"You'll sure be proud of this mare, Miss Prissy," Jeb said. "Zade is fine-blooded stock. You may have to hold her down a little. She really likes to go, and she really could, too, back in old Kaintuck."

Dozie was in the kitchen. "Come on in, Miss Prissy. Mister Doc said fix you up for the parade like I used to fix Miss Debbie."

Dozie had been Miss Debbie's own maid in Kentucky, she said. She took me into the front bedroom. It must have been Miss Debbie's room. The carpet had pink roses all over it and there were white ruffled curtains at the windows. The riding habit was laid out on the high-backed walnut bed. Dozie held it up for me to see—the long skirt, the coat with lapels like a man's, the derby hat, and a pair of shining boots.

"Nobody has ever touched these things since Miss Debbie used to wear them. Of course, I brush and air them, and Jeb greases the boots every winter."

Dozie brushed my hair and pinned it high on my head, tucking it in with little combs. She rolled the ends into curls, pinned them down at the side of my neck, and patted powder on my face from a bowl on the dresser.

"Why, child," she said as she stood back and stared. "Who'd ever thought it? You sure look like Miss Debbie— you're the spittin' image of her."

I really did look like Miss Debbie's picture. I had never had my hair done up, and it made me look like a grown lady. With a good deal of pulling and Dozie pushing I got into the boots. They were tight, but I did not mind. I could stand anything, now that I was going to ride in the parade.

Dozie fastened the long skirt and caught it up at the side. She buttoned the coat over a white scarf around my neck and pulled the derby down over my hair. She gave me two hatpins to anchor the derby and tied a face veil around it. I could not do anything but look at the strange lady in the mirror while she took a white rose from a vase and pinned it on my lapel.

"Now, here are your gloves and riding whip," she said proudly. "See, that's just the way Miss Debbie looked when she used to ride. Everything had to be just so. You look like a lady right out of a book, Miss Prissy. Nobody will ever think you are that tomboy Prissy Blake."

I went over to the long mirror between the windows. I could not believe it was I. The rusty-haired tomboy had been turned into a Cinderella girl. I did look like a lady out of a book. I had pink cheeks and a powdered nose. I winked my lashes a few times to get the effect. If I could look like that all the time, I would not mind wearing fussy clothes and pinning my hair up. I might even wear the riding habit to the picnic dinner. I looked down my nose.

"No, thank you, Mr. Governor's son," I said haughtily. "This dance is taken."

Dozie laughed until her fat sides shook. "You sure are a good play-actor, child. You better not let the men see you. You'll make every woman in this town jealous."

"Honest, Dozie? Do you think I ought to wear this? Will anyone know me?"

"They sure won't, Miss Priss. If it were not for that hair of yours being so much lighter, you would be a dead ringer for Miss Debbie. Now watch that skirt and don't stumble. Remember, you are a lady now. Hold your head high and your back straight. That's the way a lady rides."

Jeb helped me on Zade. I was not accustomed to climbing on a horse with skirts. Jeb knelt on one knee and clasped his hands together. "Now, step right on my hands, Miss Prissy, and I'll give you a foot lift." He lifted me right into the saddle.

"Jeb, you and Dozie are making a lady of me in spite of everything," I grumbled.

Old Jeb nodded. "You're a lady, all right, Miss Prissy, and don't you forget it. Of course, you'll be a tomboy until you get your growth, but you'll be all right. I'm going to watch you ride. Zade will be hard to beat."

Jeb fitted the stirrup length and I rode around the lot a few times.

"Remember, just push with your foot and pull with your knee, easy like, but watch out for Zade. She likes to run."

It was like sitting on a stool, hollowed out to fit. Riding sidesaddle was nothing at all. I could have jumped fences, too, the way I felt when Jeb opened the gate for me and I turned down the hill to the gin lot.

The floats had started out, and the riders were lining up behind them. There were dozens of men and boys dressed as cowboys and Indians. Mrs. Watts was rushing about getting things lined up. I held Zade back under a tree, away from the crowd. I saw Pinky across the lot. He was making Rummy dance sideways and pretending Rummy was a hard horse to ride. A man dressed as an Indian chief, his face painted and wearing a feathered warbonnet, rode around the lot, whooping and yelling. Zade started sidestepping. The Indian chief rode up beside me and leaned over, his painted face close to mine.

"Do I know you, girlie?" he asked. "No? Well, heap big

chief sure will before the parade's over." He gave a war whoop and rode away at a gallop.

Zade was restless; she wanted to be moving. Mrs. Watts blew her whistle like mad and pulled the riders into line almost bodily. "Line up, line up," she shrieked. The riders fell in, two by two. I still held back.

The band boys marched ahead of the floats. Boys who had puffed and tooted and banged the whole year were now in their glory, stepping along in blue coats and white pants to head the parade. Then came the mayor's carriage and the candidates for governor, each in a fancy rig. After these were the floats and horseback riders. Mrs. Watts and her senior band wound up the procession.

Just as the last rider left the lot, I pulled in ahead of the band. As I rode up to take my place, Mrs. Watts caught sight of me. She had her baton lifted to strike up the band. Her mouth fell open, and her hands dropped to her sides. She looked like a funny fat little elf, standing there in her tight blue pants and brass-buttoned coat with tight black boots on her fat legs. I waved my hand and rode out, my head high and my back straight. It was a full minute before I heard the band strike up.

We passed the blacksmith shop. People were lined up on benches and boxes and chairs before the drugstore and Brown's Drygoods. Mama would be there, in front of Brown's, looking for me. Someday I would tell her how I rode in the parade, that I was the mysterious lady of the sidesaddle, the long skirt, and the boots. The boots were tight, and my feet were beginning to swell and hurt, but it would not be for long. I could soon get them off. I heard the boys' band as it turned off toward the oil mill, four blocks down the street. Behind me Mrs. Watts and her band stamped along. Zade was feeling good. I had to hold her down, for she was prancing daintily to the music.

The Indian rider was just ahead. He turned in his saddle and called back, "That's a good nag you're on, girlie. How about racing me down Main Street?"

I ignored him and looked straight ahead. We crossed the street, and the snare drummer rolled his drum. Just as we were even with Brown's and I could see Mama's black hat with the pink ostrich tips, the band struck up again. A cowboy shouted, "Yippee—ee!" and fired his pistol into the air. In a split second Zade was off like a streak. Her leap forward threw me off balance across the saddle, but I caught and hung on by her mane, my stirruped foot sticking straight out behind me. I heard a loud war whoop, and there, riding neck and neck beside me, was the paint pony and the flying feathers of the Indian warbonnet. "Go to it, girlie," the rider yelled, "I'm right with you."

People went wild. They yelled and whistled and threw their hats into the air. "Fifty dollars on the lady," they shouted. "Fifty to ten the lady wins! Watch that girl ride!" All the way down the street the sidewalk audience was a shrieking bedlam.

Down the full length of Main Street we raced, past the cowboy and the Indian riders, past the floats, past the milling, shrieking crowds. We had passed the mayor's carriage and the boys' band on the oil-mill road before I could pull Zade in and get my balance again in the saddle. The painted Indian was right beside me, lying alongside his pony, just as I had done. He pulled up.

"Girlie," he said, panting, "you're a wonder; a real whiz. We won that money in a walk, didn't we? No one else had a chance."

I had scarcely got my breath back from the wild ride. "Well, I would not exactly call it a walk," I said.

He leaned over and peered into my face. "I didn't think you would do it. Who are you, anyway? You don't belong around here, do you?"

"No," I said shortly, and turned on up the hill.

The Indian rider followed. "Aren't you going to collect your prize money?" he asked. "The twenty-five dollars. We have to go in person."

"No, not now, and you had better not come with me," I said in my best Lady Gwendolyn manner. "My husband will be waiting for me."

"Oh," he reined in his horse. "Your husband? Well, I'll be . . ."

He turned and galloped full speed down the street toward the end of the parade.

I rode on up the hill and around to Doc Rutherford's barn lot. I was furious at the way things had turned out. The only chance I would ever have to ride in the parade, and I had spoiled it all and ridden like a wild Indian down Main Street instead of riding like a lady in Miss Debbie's riding habit. I had led the parade, all right, and I would never live it down if people found out. And they would! Gloomily I counted heads of those who knew. Too many. Pinky, for one, could not keep the secret.

Old Jeb had gone to the parade, so I unsaddled Zade and left the saddle on the block. I went on through the orchard to the house. My feet were so swollen in the tight boots that I could hardly walk. Dozie was gone, but the back door was unlocked. I went upstairs and took off Miss Debbie's riding habit—all but the boots. I pulled and tugged but could not budge them. Outside a mockingbird in a locust tree was running his scales. I had always liked mockingbirds until now, but he kept chirping, "Girlie, girlie, girlie—cheap, cheap, cheap," until I wanted to throw the boots at him. Racing down Main Street with a painted Indian—and he had called me girlie. The mockingbird was right.

I struggled with the boots until I knew there was no use. I could not get them off. I couldn't very well wear black leather riding boots with a blue dotted-swiss dress. It looked as if I would miss the picnic and the Governor and the Governor's son who went to college. Mama would be very unhappy.

"Cheap, cheap, cheap," the mockingbird jeered.

"Shut up," I shouted.

The painted china clock on the mantel struck twelve. Mama would be spreading dinner on the big table east of the speaker's stand. I thought of the coconut cake, five layers high, and the fried chicken that I would not be there to eat. "Where's Priscilla?" someone would ask. "Yes, where is Priscilla?" Mama would inquire of Pinky. And Pinky, bursting with importance, would tell her.

"Oh, didn't you know? That was Priss who just raced the Indian down Main Street."

There was water in the pitcher on the washstand. I scrubbed my face and brushed my hair and pinned braids around my head as Mama liked me to wear it. I put on my dress and sat in a chair by the window and waited. A nice exciting day ahead, with nobody around but the mockingbird and me. Everyone would be at the picnic but Priscilla Blake. Priscilla would be sitting by the window nursing her sore feet and saying things to the mockingbird.

I was just about to drop off in a doze when I heard Pinky's voice at the barn lot. Of course—Pinky had to bring Rummy back. I had forgotten.

"Pinky," I yelled. "Pinky." I ran through the orchard, but when I got to the barn, Pinky was a block down the street. He had unsaddled in double-quick time and climbed the back fence and cut across lots.

"Pinky," I shouted, "Pinky, you come back here this minute."

"I can't," he said. "I'm in a hurry."

"I said for you to come right back here, and I mean it. I need you."

"Aw, Priss, I gotta get back, I tell you." But he came. "What do you want?"

"I can't get these boots off." I sat down on the horse block.

Pinky grinned. "You sure put on a whale of a show, Sis. Whatever made you do a thing like that—racing that Indian down the street? Mama will have a fit when she knows."

"I didn't do it on purpose, and you know it. When that gun went off, Zade went off, too. There was no holding her. I guess she thought she was back at the races."

Pinky gave the tight boot such a yank that he almost took me with it as he went over backward in the dirt.

"Don't tell Mama, Pinky," I begged, "whatever you do. If you tell, I'll ask Doc not ever to let you ride Rummy again."

Pinky grinned like the imp of Satan he is. "Gosh, Priss, I won't need to tell her. The whole town will be glad to do it." He pulled off the other boot and started for the fence in a run.

"You had better keep quiet just the same," I yelled after him.

I took the boots and limped back through the orchard, the gravel cutting my sore feet through my stockings. I did not care whether I went to the picnic or not, but I was getting hungry.

Mama was cutting the coconut cake when I arrived wearing my new blue swiss. I hoped she would not notice I was wearing my old brown shoes. I had tried to get into my patent-leather pumps, but they would not go on. Judge Harper, the man Mama hoped would be governor, was holding out his plate.

"I saved room for the cake, Mrs. Blake," he said. "Even as good as that fried chicken was, I remembered how good your cake is."

I looked at the heap of chicken bones on his plate. From

the looks of them, he could not have saved much room. Then I looked at Judge Harper. From the looks of him, there should be plenty of room. I slipped into a vacant place near the end of the table, hoping Mama would not see me, but she did. Judge Harper's plate was waiting. "Priscilla," she said, "I missed you on the float. Where have you been?"

Somebody beside me put fried chicken on my plate and pushed a bowl of potato salad into my hands. I was so starved I could have hugged him.

"Oh, I just didn't get dressed in time. It was a long walk and too hot to hurry."

More food kept coming from my left, and I turned to see who was bringing up the reinforcements. A dark-haired young man with nice brown eyes and very white teeth smiled at me, then shoveled some pickles onto my plate.

"Eat now and don't talk, girlie," he said.

"Girlie!" I dropped my drumstick and stared. So that's who it was!

He grinned and winked. "You're okay, however many husbands you have," he whispered.

"Oh, Priscilla," Mama said coyly, "I was about to forget to introduce you to our guests. Governor Harper, this is my daughter, Priscilla."

"And this is my son, Richard," boomed the Judge.

Richard rose and bowed low over my hand, like Sir Walter Raleigh at the mudhole. "Where's the husband?" he murmured with a slight leer.

"I just murdered him," I said under my breath, "and I'm about ready for another one."

"Another husband? Swell. I am glad I'm here."

"No, idiot, another murder," I hissed. "Now shut up."

"Thank you," he said aloud. "It's just as I hoped." He turned his wonderful smile on Mama, who beamed right

back at him. "Mrs. Blake, I do hope Priscilla is as good a
cook as you are. If she is, she will make some man a perfect wife. I have never eaten such wonderful food."

Mama fluttered and looked pleased. "I hope you choke,"
I said.

Richard patted my hand. "Priscilla is such a little lady,
Mrs. Blake, and I do like sweet, helpless girls."

I kicked his ankle under the table. "Can't you shut up?"
I whispered.

The Judge was booming away, and I had to look up and
smile. "Richard takes after his father," he said. "He's a
ladies' man, Miss Priscilla. As a matter of fact, I'm not too
old myself to look at a pretty girl, and believe me, I'm looking." And believe me, he was.

"If you're through eating, Priscilla," Mama said, almost
purring, "show Richard around. I won't need you."

I rose, groaning.

"Oh, Priscilla," Mama called. "Did anyone find out who
that awful woman was who raced the drunken Indian down
the street? Such a shameless thing to do."

"No, Mama, I didn't," I said. "I came straight here from
home."

"Oh, those two?" Richard answered her as he slid his
hand under my elbow. "I know the fellow. He's really a very
extraordinary person and he wasn't drunk at all—just high
spirited. And he wasn't an Indian. But the lady—you would
really be surprised to know who she was. She's . . ."

"Come on, Richard, let's go see the balloon ascension."

"What! No coconut cake? It's delicious."

"No, no cake," I said through my clenched teeth. "All I
want is to push you into the deepest well I can find."

"Aw, let's go turn over a buggy instead," he whispered.

Chapter 6

*T*he Weekly Index *came out on Friday, the day after* the parade. In big type, on the front page, were the names of the prizewinners. My name, like Abou Ben Adhem's, led all the rest. "Priscilla Blake, best woman rider, wins $25.00; Richard Harper, best man rider, wins $25.00." Beneath the names was the story.

Everyone read the *Weekly Index.* It was our only scandal sheet. I felt exactly like the woman who had the scarlet letter sewed on her jerkin. You would have thought there had been a funeral in the house after the paper came, for it was Mama's first inkling of my part in the parade. I had not felt equal to telling her.

"To think this should happen to my daughter," she wailed, and went to bed with cold cloths on her head. Pinky bounced around like a chicken with its head off, gloating over the race, asking how I would spend the money, saying he could buy those goatskin chaps for ten dollars, and glooming over Mama's edict that she never wanted to hear anyone speak of riding a horse again.

I wanted to see Doc. I slipped out the side gate and took the short cut to his house, but he was not at home. The back door was locked, and I knew that Dozie had gone, too. I went on to the barn lot, but it was deserted. Jeb had taken the horses back to the pasture.

I went back home and put on the old riding pants and filled my pockets with tea cakes. I stuffed my hair under one of Pinky's caps and went through the orchard to the spring. I liked to sit there under the big cottonwood tree and read or lie on the grass and watch the Gulf clouds move slowly across the sky. Clouds always helped me out of a bad mood. It did something to me to watch the great white masses, piled up like snowbanks in the sky. I always came away feeling better.

After the cookies were gone and I felt peaceful again, I decided to go down across the adjoining field to the Walters' orchard. There would be plenty of late peaches and yellow apples there. As I turned into the lane leading to the orchard, I heard a woman screaming. The screams came from a little two-room house at the lower end of the lane, where a cotton-picking outfit had camped. In the fall of the year families of cotton pickers drifted in, moving south with the sun, and camped in vacant shacks along the edge of town. They stayed for the picking season and moved on, traveling in rickety wagons pulled by thin, shabby teams. And the people were as thin and shabby as their teams. Their belongings consisted of a roll of ragged bedding, an old cookstove, a few dishes, two or three chairs, and some cooking utensils.

I arrived breathless at the open door and called "Hello."

A gaunt woman, her eyes red with weeping, came to the door. Her thin shoulders were shaking as if from a hard chill. "She's going to die," she shrieked. "She's dying right now. Oh, Lordy, help me—help me in my tribulations."

A young girl lay huddled on a pile of ragged quilts on the floor. Her face was white and drawn. Her eyes had the terrified, defiant look of a wounded animal. She moaned softly through clenched teeth.

"I'll get a doctor," I said. I was scared. I had never seen anyone look so hurt and helpless. "She's pretty sick."

"No, no, you can't get a doctor," the woman whispered hoarsely. "She's going to have a baby, and she's not married."

"Just the same, she needs a doctor," I said. "How long has she been like this?"

The woman sat down in an old sagging chair and wiped her eyes with a shaking hand. "I don't know," she said dully. "I was asleep. She just took, I think."

I ran all the way to the lower end of the lane, where it cut out into the country road, thinking I might meet a buggy or wagon and get a ride back to town, but no one was in sight. The air was filled with dust raised by some vehicle that had passed, and my feet stirred up more. I could hardly breathe.

I jogged on, thinking of the frightened girl on the ragged quilts. My throat hurt, and my eyes stung. She had looked no older than I, and she was going to have a baby. It scared me, and I felt ashamed—ashamed for myself and for Mama and the whole town. We all thought the picnic and parade the most important things in town, and here this girl lay on ragged quilts, about to have a baby, and the only food in sight was half a sack of flour on the bare kitchen table. I could not run any faster, so I prayed for someone to come by.

A buggy drove up and stopped. I looked up to see the new preacher, Mr. Whitlock. I had seen him only once or twice, at a distance, for we did not go to his church.

"Going to town, son?" he asked. "Do you want a lift?"

"Oh, yes, Mr. Whitlock," I said, strangling from the dust. "I've got to get a doctor quick. A girl's having a baby over there in the flat."

The Reverend Mr. Whitlock stared at me in astonishment. "What does this mean?" he asked. "A young boy like you mixed up with trash. Who is this girl?"

"Why, Mr. Whitlock, I'm Priscilla Blake." I pulled my cap off, and my hair fell over my shoulders. "The girl is in that house up the lane. Only her mother is with her, and she's scared crazy. They need a doctor quick."

Mr. Whitlock stopped the horse and took out his glasses. He put them on with shaking hands and looked me over, then turned brick red and chewed his sandy moustache. "You're Mrs. Thomas Blake's daughter?" he asked sternly.

"Yes, sir, I am."

"Well," he said with chilling disapproval, "I am taking you home to your mother right now. You should know better than to get mixed up with trash like that, and you should not be wandering around these flats alone at your age. It is no place for a girl."

"But, Mr. Whitlock," I protested, "we'll have to get a doctor first. The baby is on its way. It is probably almost here."

"Hush!" He was horrified by my brazen manner. A girl did not speak of such things, even to her mother. And to a preacher? Never!

He looked me over, frowning. "Running around in pants, and you almost a woman grown. I am going to write a sermon on this new generation." He punched out his lower lip and slapped the horse hard with the reins.

Mr. Whitlock took me home and deposited me in my mother's care. "Mrs. Blake, I have brought your daughter home. I found her—" he glared at me—"like this!"

Mama took one look at my dusty, tear-streaked face and turned pale. "Oh," she whispered, her eyes big and frightened, "what has she done?"

Mr. Whitlock folded his arms and looked at me accusingly. "Some trashy girl in the flat is sick. She's—er—ah—"

"She's having a baby, Mama, and she needs a doctor."

"Hush, Priscilla," Mama whispered and looked warningly toward the parlor door.

"Yes, your daughter has been there," Mr. Whitlock said heatedly. "I want to have a talk with you, Mrs. Blake. Your daughter is in need of religious counsel."

"Why, Mr. Whitlock," Mama said, stiffening, "Priscilla goes regularly to Sunday school and church."

"That's just it. I'm going to write a sermon—"

"Please, not now," I begged. "Get a doctor quick. The girl will die, and the baby will die."

Mama pushed me toward the stairs. "Run on up and get dressed, Priscilla," she whispered. "Mr. Whitlock, I'll be pleased to see you another time. I am sure you want to get a doctor now."

Mr. Whitlock left.

"Mama, that woman needs help, and the girl needs a doctor. I want to go back and help her."

"I am sure Mr. Whitlock will see that they get a doctor and any help they need. It really is no place for you. Besides, you have company." She shook her head. "You do look like a dirty little street urchin. But hurry and wash and get into a nice dress."

I watched Mr. Whitlock drive away in his buggy. He headed east on Main Street. There was no doctor in that direction. I turned and saw a straw sailor-hat with a dotted band perched on the hall tree. Then I knew. That accounted for the paint pony tied out in front.

"Hurry, Priscilla," Mama whispered. "Richard Harper is in the parlor looking at the stereoscope views. Do be nice to him. I asked him to stay for supper."

I was in no mood to be nice to anyone, least of all to Richard Harper.

"But, Mama, that girl—that poor girl—" But Mama had disappeared into the kitchen.

The paint pony tried to buck me off all the way up the hill to Doc's house. I had never ridden a bucking horse before, nor a saddle with a horn, but I hung on and was glad for the horn. He was mean and hardmouthed, but he was fast. I had heard Richard shouting as I started off, but I kept going.

Doc was just pulling away in his buggy as I rode up. I slipped off, relieved that I had found him, and tied the sweating horse, still jerking at the bit, to Doc's hitching post. Richard would follow and find him there. I told Doc about the girl, and he frowned. "Jump in," he said. "You will have to help. I have another patient almost as bad, but she can wait. She's an old hand. I've helped her with five."

"Do you think I'd better go, Doc? Mama wouldn't like it, and she has a beau waiting for me."

"Hell's little fishes! Of course you had better go," Doc snorted. "Get in."

It was almost dark when I got home again. Doc had gone on to his other patient, and I cut across the field and up by the spring to the orchard path.

Mama did not scold me, but she looked very downcast and worried.

"Richard said you went off with Doc, and I knew. I didn't tell him where. He was scared to death when he saw you riding the paint. That horse killed a man, and he's not safe. Priscilla, it just took all the starch out of me. And after yesterday—" she moaned. "Why do you do things like that?"

I was so tired that my whole body ached and my feet felt like lead. My brain was tired, and I could not think. I could only see pictures—the girl on the pallet bed, the clean sheets Doc gave them. He always carried them for folks not as lucky as he. And the weeping mother whom we left smiling and crooning to a tiny pink baby wrapped in a square of old table linen.

"We'll get clothes to you later," Doc promised the woman. "But don't bother about dressing either of them now. They are both tired, and sleep is all they need."

It had been like a dream—a strange confused dream of brand new experiences that kept my brain racing to keep up with what I had to do. But I no longer felt guilty or ashamed. In spite of my weariness, I was glad and happy inside.

Mr. Banner had come from his cotton-picking just as we were leaving. He was a thin, stooped, tired little man, his blue eyes red-rimmed and watery.

"After you've had your supper, Banner," Doc said, "go into town and find my house. Anyone can tell you where it is. Tell my cook to give you food, food for a sick woman. She'll know. The girl will need it tomorrow."

Mr. Banner wiped his forehead with his faded shirt sleeve. "I shore appreciate all this, Doc," he said, gulping. "I'll collect for my pickin' Saturday night, and I kin——"

Doc picked up his bag. "Keep your money, Banner. You'll need it later on."

The pictures were flashing off and on in my brain like heat lightning. I remembered I was home again, standing by the parlor window and Mama wanting to know why I did things like riding Richard Harper's killer horse.

"I had to get Doc; that's why. The girl needed him."

"But I would have gone with him, Priscilla. It was no place for a girl like you," Mama moaned. "You should have come for me."

"No, you couldn't go." I dragged the heavy lumps that were my feet to the stairs. "You had to fix supper for Richard."

"Well," she said sadly, "you'll not see Richard again. Not after this."

There were long steps to climb, and I did not answer.

Papa came in just before supper. "I want to see the notorious Prissy Blake," he said. "She's the talk of the country. I heard about the parade before I got to the Washita River."

"I'll never live over it," Mama said, grieving. "Priscilla is disgraced. Everybody was already talking about her, and she's just out of that disgrace and into another."

Papa grinned and winked at me over Mama's head. "What else, for Pete's sake?"

Well, there she was, Mama told him, hiding at home, ashamed to show her face after the parade, when in comes the new preacher, bringing me home dressed in pants. The preacher had picked me up some place in the flat with a story about a girl having a baby. And I had gone back with Doctor Rutherford to that place, with Richard Harper waiting in the parlor.

Papa told Mama it was all right. He could not see that I had done anything so bad. What if I had ridden in the parade? It had not hurt anyone. "It's a darn shame," he said, "that Zade had to revert to her racing days, but I would have given twenty-five dollars to have seen it."

But her going off with Doc like that. It was no place for a girl, Mama said.

"I'm proud of her for it, Sally. That poor girl had to have a doctor, and Doc would not take Priss anywhere she should not go. After all, Priss is seventeen. As for that preacher— well, if he stays around here, he may learn a few things."

I went with Papa to help unharness the buckskins. When he had hung away the harness he said, "How would you like to have a horse of your own, Priss?"

Papa knew I wanted a horse more than anything, so I

just went on currying Buckshot. Papa had run across a
filly up in the Choctaw country. "It's the prettiest piece of
horseflesh you could find in a day's ride. It's a palomino,
the first I have ever seen—more gold color than the buckskins and a lighter tail. When that little filly is broken to
ride, she will run circles around any horse in this area—
and there are some pretty good ones, you know."

"Oh, tell me more." I was excited, but I knew it took
money to buy horses, sometimes as much as seventy-five
dollars, and we did not have it to spare.

"You could ride beside the queen on that filly, and nobody
would look at the queen, Priss," Papa went on. "They would
be watching your horse."

"But when do I get her?"

"Well," Papa said, "I told Joe Edwards, who owns her,
that if he would wait a while for the money, I would try
to figure something out. Something will turn up, Priss. It
always does."

Chapter 7

On Sunday afternoon Papa was reading the newspaper on the front porch when Mr. Brending, our school principal, opened the gate and came in.

"Tom Blake, you are just the man I want to see," Mr. Brending said. "I hoped I would find you home."

Papa offered him a chair, but Mr. Brending said he would just sit on the steps with me, and he would take a glass of that lemonade.

"Tom, you surely missed the best show this town ever had," he said. "Never in my life have I seen anything to equal Prissy's ride down Main Street." He laughed until I wanted to leave. "Don't go, Priss," he begged. "I wish I could have done it myself. Besides, my business with your father may interest you."

Mr. Brending set down his empty glass. "I have a proposition, Tom. I don't know how you will take it, but it's this. Page Carter told me Thursday that they need a teacher

for a run-down school near him. It is a government school
and will pay fifty dollars a month. I thought maybe Priss
could try her hand at teaching."

Papa twirled his watch chain and looked at me, his eyes
barely open. "Seventy-five dollars would buy that filly.
Think you could do it, Priss?"

"Papa, I would swim Red River with my hands tied behind me for a chance at that filly," I said. "I really would."

Papa grunted. "Swimming Red River might be easier;
that country is pretty tough; but swimming the river
wouldn't pay as well."

"Then it's settled?" Mr. Brending asked. "I told Page I
would ask you about it. He said they would board Priss."

"No, it won't be settled until we talk to her mother. She
has pretty strong ideas about some things. But we'll see."

Mama put her foot down promptly on the teaching proposition. Filly or no filly, no daughter of hers would teach
school in that wild Indian country. And even if the Indians
did not scalp people anymore and it was not Custer's last
stand, there was never any telling when they might break
out again.

Papa laughed. "Sally, I have been driving up and down the
Canadian in the Choctaw country for years. The only Indians Priss will likely see will be wearing peg-top pants or
Gibson-girl shirtwaists. The Indians send their children to
college now, and they are not half as wild as a lot of these
smart alecks tearing around Lynwood."

"But Priscilla is only seventeen," Mama said. "She's much
too young to be on her own."

Papa tilted Mama's chin so he could look into her eyes.
"Sally, how old were you when you married me and came
West with me? Sixteen, wasn't it?"

Mama flushed and picked up her sewing. "Don't run
away," Papa said. "You have been worrying your head off

because Priss is a tomboy. Let her get away and look after herself for a few months. It will be good for her."

When Mama finally calmed down, she began planning the clothes I should have. Mama firmly believed that teaching a country school was hazardous and that my chances of being captured by the Indians were more than good. But if I were going to be, she apparently reasoned, she would see that I was properly clothed for the occasion.

Had I been preparing for a wedding and honeymoon at Niagara Falls, I would not have had more clothes. "But why a dozen petticoats?" I groaned. "You know I won't wear them." I hated to spend my hard-earned money for such foolishness. I had told Mama to charge the materials and I would pay for them out of my first check. "Can't I be enough of a lady with the clothes I wear in Lynwood?"

Mama turned pale at the thought. "You teach school with dresses halfway to your knees?" she asked, shocked. "If the trustees saw you with your stockings showing, you would probably lose your school. It is bad enough for you to run around Lynwood in short dresses and only one petticoat, but you will certainly have to be more properly dressed if you expect to be a schoolteacher."

Mama set me to ripping lace from her old petticoat flounces. "The lace is still good," she said. "Your grandma crocheted it, and it is a shame not to use it again. We'll put it on your nightgowns."

"The trustees won't see me in my nightgowns, will they?"

Mama turned green around her mouth. "Priscilla Blake," she said scoldingly through yards of white material she was measuring, "you are my only daughter, and it isn't my fault that you are a tomboy." She picked up the scissors and started slashing away at the material. "But there's one thing certain. If you and your father have made up your minds that you are going to teach that school, you must act and dress like a lady."

I had two weeks to get ready for the school opening. Mama passed around dress goods to all the neighbors who had volunteered to sew for me. Meanwhile she went into a whirlwind session with her sewing machine and the white goods. Mama seemed to think that what I lacked in the appurtenances of a lady could be made up for by the number and yardage of flounced petticoats I possessed. Judging from the number, it took a lot of petticoats to balance the appurtenances I did not have.

I considered my future with gloomy foreboding. I wanted the palomino filly more than I had ever wanted anything, but it would come high if I had to wear all the clothes that were being made for me. But Mama had laid down the law. There was nothing else to do but to bow down and submit to the shackles of womanhood—the flounced petticoats, high-buttoned shoes, and worst of all, a corset. Only a horse and saddle were worth it, and there were times I was not sure they were.

Pinky thought the petticoats were a wonderful joke. But when he found Mama had bought me a corset, Pinky acted as if that miserable thing were a suit of linked mail. One afternoon I found Pinky and practically every boy in the neighborhood in my room. Pinky had on my corset over his shirt and knickers and was taking the other boys on, one at a time, in a fencing match with umbrellas.

"Oh, gee, why do you have to spoil everything?" Pinky grumbled as I ran them out. "Just because you're going to be an old schoolteacher, you don't have to be such an old grouch. Next thing you know, you'll have a beau. Ho, ho, ho, Priss will catch a beau," he chanted as he jumped out of my reach and ran.

Chapter 8

I was up and dressed early for my trip to Oak Grove, not in the old dress I wanted to wear but in the green-plaid skirt and white shirtwaist that Mama thought was appropriate for meeting school trustees. And, of course, my corset.

Papa had gone out to harness the team to the road buggy. "We had better start early," he said. "We have a long drive ahead, and with last night's rain we might run into some muddy roads. You are lucky," he added, "to be able to stay with the Carters, the only house in the area that has an extra bedroom."

I was glad for the room to myself but would have shared a shed with the Carter cow to own the palomino.

Pinky struggled with the straps of the trunk. "Priss," he yelled, "you will have to come down and sit on this thing and bounce. It won't shut."

I went down and sat and bounced, but nothing happened.

"Ha, there's a curse on it," Pinky snarled.

"There is nothing wrong with the trunk. It is simply too full of clothes. With corsets to bind me and petticoats to hobble me, I must be punished by teaching a bunch of young hyenas like you who will never learn grammar."

"Well, throw away the petticoats; throw away the old corset. You won't wear it."

"But I am wearing it," I said sweetly.

Pinky's freckled face shone like a turkey egg, and his eyes went blank but only for a fleeting instant. He dived at me and stabbed me with his finger, right in my stomach, to see if I really did have on the corset. I doubled up, and fell off the trunk.

Suddenly Mama burst through the door from the kitchen. "Oh," she gasped and disappeared into her bedroom. In a minute she was back again. "To think I almost forgot them." She thrust a package into my hands. "Here, Priscilla, they're for you." Her eyelashes were wet and her eyes ready to brim over. Mama was one of those rare women who are even prettier when they cry.

I was holding my breath. I wanted a pair of leather gauntlets with fringe and red stars on the cuffs.

The present was not leather gauntlets. It was a pair of long red-silk gloves, the first long gloves I had ever seen.

"See, they're the very latest fashion. They are called elbow gloves," she said proudly. Mr. Brown just got them in from St. Louis."

I was so disappointed I nearly cried.

"Mama, will you tell me what use I will have for these where I am going?" I asked, laying the gloves on the trunk.

Mama picked up the red gloves and held them up before her. "I can just see you wearing these, Priscilla, with those elbow-sleeved shirtwaists I made for you. Men do so like red gloves," she sighed.

Pinky snatched at the gloves. "Ho, ho, catch a beau,"

he shouted. "Red gloves are beau catchers. Old maid Priss will catch a beau."

In three shakes I had Pinky on his knees yelling "Quit!" It was a jujitsu trick I had learned from the boys. I stuffed the gloves into a corner of the trunk, hoping never to see them again. Such foolish money Mama had spent. And I had wanted fringed gauntlets.

Just then Papa came in. "All ready, Priss?" he asked. "How about the trunk?" He closed and strapped it. "What in thunderation have you got in it—bricks?"

Mama cried when I left, and even Pinky looked sober and didn't kick at me when I kissed him goodbye.

When we got to the main road, we drove along at a pretty fast clip. There had been a hard rain in the night, and the puddles in the wheel ruts sent up little splashes as the wheels cut through them. The air was good and fresh with the faint wild smell of ripening seed-pods and the bitter tang of sumac and thistles. Small cottony clouds, left behind by the rainstorm, had been washed clean and hung up in the blue to dry.

After several days in the lot the buckskins wanted to go. The muscles in their creamy flanks worked like pistons on an engine. "We will get there in a hurry at this rate," I said, and leaned back to enjoy the fresh breeze.

"Probably it is a good thing you did pack your trunk with bricks or we would not even hit the ground except in high places," Papa said, chuckling. "These ponies can sure split the breeze when I let them out. I never take the whip out of the socket."

The perfectly matched buckskins stepped together like dancers, their small, neat hooves lifting and setting down as precisely as in a minuet. Suddenly it came over me that every minute I was going farther and farther from home. The joys and fun of my growing-up years were all over. No longer would Pinky and I ride Doc's horses around the pasture bareback and without a bridle. My corset stays pinched my stomach, my high collar stuck my neck, and my head was sore where I had twisted my hair so tight. I was getting gloomier every wheel's turn when Papa patted my hand.

"Buck up, Priss," he said, trying to comfort me. "Think of that filly. You are going to own the finest saddle horse in the territory. Think you can ride her?"

"Can I ride her? You know I can, Papa. Just give me a chance. When will I get her?" The three months ahead seemed like three years.

"Joe's breaking her now. He is going to break her to skirts, he said." Papa cut his eyes around toward me and grinned. "I told Joe we were having a hard enough time breaking you to skirts, and I figured you would rather he didn't. But he said you would get around to skirts sooner or later, so he would just go ahead and make a lady's mare out of her."

I laughed. "I didn't do so well with skirts at the parade, did I?"

"You didn't do so bad either," Papa answered.

He dug into his pocket for his pipe and sucked at the stem, handing me the reins. "You drive while I smoke. I will have enough driving when I start home."

Papa had never let me drive the buckskins before. I pulled off my gloves and stuffed them into my pocket. They had wool in them, and reins slip through wool like silk. That reminded me of the red-silk gloves.

"Papa," I said, exploding, "I wanted fringed leather gauntlets, and what do you think Mama bought for me?"

Papa laughed. "Probably a peekaboo shirtwaist? Or maybe a fantail skirt? Something to make a lady out of you for sure, Priss."

"Red gloves," I said in disgust. "Red-silk elbow gloves!"

Papa whooped. "Red-silk gloves? For you, Priss? Well,

you had better watch out. Red gloves are beau catchers, they say. You will be bringing home a beau first crack out of the box."

"I will not," I declared, and gave the buckskins a smart slap with the reins. As if they had been waiting for just that signal, the team was off like scared jackrabbits. Down the flat prairie road they went in a hard run, the light buggy bouncing in the ruts and my trunk banging the springs at every jolt. I tried to shove the reins into Papa's hands. "They're running away!"

Papa folded his arms. "You're driving, Priss," he said indifferently. "Keep your head. You gave them the reins, and they took them. Before you try to manage horses, Priss, you have to know their tricks. The trouble is, these ponies know a poor helpless woman is driving them."

Poor helpless woman! Fiddlesticks! I might have to wear starched petticoats and red-silk elbow gloves, but I was not helpless. I was so angry I sawed the reins hard.

Papa whistled. "Why, Priss, I'm ashamed of you. You know you can ruin a horse's mouth that way. Just work up on your reins. Steady now, and a little more to the right. Circle them on that smooth strip of prairie. They will soon get their run out and be glad to stop."

The ponies were circling back to the road again. I had my feet on the dashboard; my hair was down and blowing in my face. My hat was gone, but I did not care. I had stopped the runaway buckskins, and I felt great.

"Head them back down the road the way we came, and we'll pick up your hat. Now remember this, Priss. Always drive with a light rein but steady, and don't take sudden fits of temper out on the horses. You will find this system works with men as well as with horses."

Mrs. Carter was waiting supper for us. She was a plump, nearsighted little woman with reddish hair, gold-rimmed

glasses, and a pleasant gold-toothed smile. Page Carter was
not as big as Papa, but he was hard-muscled and brown
as a nut. His dark eyes twinkled when he saw me all rigged
out in my flounced skirt and high-collared shirtwaist.

"Why, Tom, are you right sure this is the girl who won
the race? Hi, Priss," he said, grinning. I knew instantly
I need not wear dignified clothes to impress Page Carter.

"She's the girl," Papa said. "Her mother's trying to make
a lady out of her now, and it's a little hard on her. I am
not too much against her being a lady, but see she does not
get it in too big doses. Let her ride now and then, and she
will be happy."

"I thought of that," Page answered. "I have a little chestnut mare named Daisy. Priss can ride her from Friday
night to Monday morning if she wants."

I could have hugged Page.

After Papa left early Sunday morning, I went to my
room to unpack. Mrs. Carter came in and settled herself
in the rocking chair.

"I'll just set and rest while you shake out your things,"
she said cheerfully. "Your pa told me that all your ma's
done for the past two weeks was to make tucks and ruffles
for you."

The rockers clicked on and off the braided rug while
Hetty talked.

"I told Page it was a mistake bringing you here. Not
that I'm not glad to have you, but sure as the world, you
are going to run into trouble. Preacher Higgins is dead set
against women teachers."

I unfolded my best flounced petticoat. "Why didn't they
get a man, then?"

"They can't." Hetty leaned forward to examine the embroidery. "Say, that's sure pretty," she said. "The boys
always run the teachers off, that's why. They can't find

a man to take it." She sighed and slowed down her rocking. "I used to have pretty things like that before I married. I made them myself. But you sure give up a lot when you marry. It takes so much time to wash and iron for a man."

Hetty's round, unlined face was the picture of contentment. Her hair was smooth and neat, and her gray Sunday calico, sprigged with rosebuds, had a frill at the neck. She was tidy as a pin.

"You don't look as if you gave up quite everything," I said, laughing. "I'll bet you would not trade back, now would you?"

She smiled and rocked. "No, I don't expect I would." She turned up the hem of her dress to show a plain unbleached-muslin underskirt. "That's what I wear now. I have no use for the ruffled ones, but I guess you will have to wear yours for the preacher."

"What's the preacher got to do with my wearing petticoats?" I asked.

"He's head trustee, Prissy. I told Page he ought not let the preacher boss things so. It's hard on the teachers, him sneaking in and out the way he does and them not expecting him."

A nice prospect. Preacher Higgins and the bad boys waiting to run me off. Well, let them try. I would wear trailing skirts and three ruffled petticoats if that was what the old ogre wanted, but I would teach that school. Papa had said I could pay for my clothes and that palomino filly in three months, and for three months I could stand anything.

"Let him sneak about if he wants," I said. "I came here to teach school, and he is not going to run me off."

Hetty shook her head doubtfully. When she left to start dinner, I put the preacher out of my mind. I wanted to go to the horse lot and look at the chestnut mare.

Page was saddling his horse, a big nervous bay. The little mare was a pretty thing, gentle as could be, but frisky. I knew I would like her.

"I am just going to run the cows out of the corn in that patch across the creek," Page told me. "If you want to go, the mare's bridle is hanging just inside the shed there. She has a saddle, but Tom tells me you don't need a saddle."

I held out my flounced skirt. "But I can't ride in this thing, Page."

Page chuckled. "I guess not. Climb into the granary, and you'll find a pair of pants hanging on a nail. Punk Willard left them. He's a dried-up little possum, and his britches should just about fit you."

I must have looked pretty funny with a ruffled shirt-waist and worn-out pants because Page called Hetty to come and see.

Page whacked Daisy on the flanks with his old white-felt hat. She almost jumped from under me.

"Whoop-ee-ee," Page yelled. "Sic 'em, Tige."

Off we went at a hard run down the wagon road to the west field, Page whooping, Tige barking, and Daisy and I bringing up the rear. The September sun was hot overhead, but the breeze was fresh. If living in the backwoods was like this, I loved it already.

Chapter 9

I *had finished breakfast and gone to my room to gird my-*self in corset and petticoats for my first day of school when Hetty called out to me that Dora Brock, one of my pupils, had come to walk to school with me. "Anything you want to know, just ask Dora," Hetty said. "If she doesn't know, nobody will."

Dora was a thin-legged child of about eight. Her patched cotton dress was starched and fresh from the iron. A ruffled pink-calico sunbonnet rode proudly on tightly braided loops of sandy hair under which her face, lightly sprinkled with freckles, was shining clean. Her intelligent blue eyes and eager, friendly manner were comforting. I appreciated comfort in this hour of need.

"I figured you'd not know the way, and Pappy said I'd best show you," she announced when Hetty had introduced us.

Dora looked me over. "You're sure dressed up mighty fine,

59

Miss Prissy," she said. "We never had no woman teacher before. I'm glad you come. I like to look at purty clothes."

"Well, maybe you'll have some pretty clothes someday." The straight little cotton was clean as soap and water could make it, but it was not pretty.

"No'm, I don't expect to. We're too pore. I do well to have cotton checks," she said. "I'll bet your Ma's proud of you. You look so nice."

Mama would have been proud of me because I looked so much like a schoolteacher. Even Hetty had been impressed with the neat blue jumper and the elbow-sleeved shirt-waist. I had braided my hair and pinned it high on my head.

We walked the sandy road that twisted and turned through the post-oak timber. Dora chattered about the weather, the crops, the school, and the people. In the still September morning we could hear the rusty sawing of a locust and the occasional whack of a landing grasshopper.

"Are there any blanket Indians around here?" I asked. I knew, of course, there were not, but I liked to hear Dora talk.

"Sakes alive, no. I been living here since I was borned, and they never have been any around here. 'Cept Page Carter, of course, but he don't count."

"Page Carter an Indian?" Papa had never mentioned that.

"'Course. That's the reason he's got all that land." Dora detoured to examine a clump of dried grass at the roots of an old stump and held up an empty egg shell. "See, it were a potteridge's nest, but they're gone away now. I saw the old un once. She tried to trail me away, draggin' her wing, but I found the nest. 'Course, I didn't touch it—you can't touch a potteridge's nest whilst she's settin', or the hen'll leave. Pappy said so."

We crossed a dry creek and climbed a little rise. "Pappy said if he'd had sense to marry Indian blood, we'd be wearin' store-boughten clothes, too. Mammy said she shore wished he had, and she coulda done the same. But I guess it was a good thing they didn't. I don't know whose young un I'd a been."

A weed-grown wagon trail branched off the road and lost itself in a scrub of sumac bushes. Sounds of dogs barking, hens cackling, and a mule braying in the distance broke the stillness.

"Is that Old MacDonald's farm?" I asked, humming the old song.

"No'm, that's where the Hatters outfit lives," Dora said, sniffing. "Them Hatters boys is meaner'n the old Scratch 'fore day. Zeke's not mean, but he's puny, and the others pick on him. Mammy says if the other boys don't kill him afore he's grown, it'll be the Lord's blessing. They're that bad. They'll cause you trouble, Miss Prissy, sure as everything."

"I am not afraid of boys, Dora."

"Well, I betcha never run into a passel like these uns. Pappy said any teacher could hold the Hatters boys a month ought to get a whole row of brass buttons for pure spunk." Dora sighed wistfully. "He said he reckon no woman can do it, but Mammy said she shore wished she could try her hand at it. I hope you can do it, Miss Prissy, 'cause I shore want you to stay."

There had been some pretty tough boys in Lynwood, but I knew most of their tricks. The meanest were usually big bluffs. I was not afraid of the Hatters outfit. I might have to wear starched petticoats to please Mama and Preacher Higgins, but any bad boy who ran me off would have to get up pretty early in the morning.

"Don't worry about the boys, Dora. You help me, and I'll stay," I promised.

Dora stopped at a clump of bushes and took a big clasp knife out of her pocket. "Pappy said I'd best bring it along. He figured you'd need some good switches to start off with."

"But I am not going to whip anyone, Dora."

"Well, you'd best have them, just the same. Pappy said folks ain't near so likely to try to outsmart you if you've got handy what it takes to lick 'em. He told me to cut you a handful of whups that'd raise whelps on a wildcat. It's too wet to pick cotton, and the Hatters boys will be out full swing."

"You mean 'welts,' Dora, not 'whelps,' " I corrected her. "Whelps are the wildcat's kittens."

"Well, cat or kittens, you'll need whups for the Hatters," Dora insisted dryly.

Around a turn in the road we came face to face with the schoolhouse, a little log building in a grass-grown clearing. It was not actually a clearing, for there were no stumps. No trees had ever grown there. It was as if the post-oak timber had worn itself out climbing the ridge and stopped to rest, then passed on, forgetting the open space it had left behind.

It was such a little log house. If it had been on wheels, I could almost have pulled it away on a string. It sat squarely in the middle of the clearing, staring at us out of two broken-paned windows, as if it were embarrassed at its down-at-the-heels appearance. The roof was covered with scrappy shingles, and a rusty tin flue was perched on the center of the ridgepole. Someone had tried a patching job on the windows with boards, but the boards had apparently run out. A nice breezy prospect for September, but when the rains started and the northers came, it would not be so pleasant.

"That's it, Miss Prissy." Dora peered at me anxiously. At the sight of the school I had stopped stone still. Papa had said the building would not be much, but I had not expected this pathetic little shack, which looked like a deserted corncrib. So much chinking had fallen out from between the logs that you could have shot deer through the open spaces.

"You reckon you'll like it?" Dora asked, gulping, "with your fine clothes?"

"I'll like it," I said grimly.

There could not have been a worse school building in the whole Indian Territory. The worst and the least—but it was mine. Forlorn as the situation was, the sun was warm, it was not raining, and Joe Edwards was breaking my palomino filly to skirts. I marched to the door and pushed it open. The one hinge pulled loose. I caught the door as it fell and with Dora's help propped it against the wall.

"Well, we won't need a door today, anyway," I said. "Besides, I may have to make a quick exit."

The inside was even more discouraging. The floor of cottonwood planks had warped over the years, leaving cracks almost wide enough for a child to step through. It was littered with dried mud and ashes.

"Dora, this is awful," I said, groaning. "Isn't someone supposed to clean this schoolroom?"

"Yes'm," Dora answered soberly. "That's the teacher's job. But I'll help, Miss Prissy."

An unpainted table on a low platform was my desk. Back of this was a straight-backed bench. Three planks, about twelve inches wide and six feet long, were painted black and nailed against the log wall. That was the blackboard. The benches were roughly built and rickety. Even with the heavy iron stove, which stood on wooden blocks in the center of the schoolhouse, the room could never be warm in cold weather. It was not fit for a horse stall, yet I was expected to teach in it.

Flecks and splashes of sunshine streamed through the broken chinking, painting a cheerful polka-dot pattern in the dust. Locusts were fiddling away happily outside, and a little breeze wandered in, loaded with woodsy odors. I lifted my head, and a defiant feeling of pride and achievement took over. This was my school. Somewhere up there in Washington my name was on some paper—Priscilla Blake, teacher, Oak Grove School, Indian Territory. I was a government schoolteacher. But only for a moment did the proud feeling last. I suddenly realized there was not a pupil in sight except Dora.

"I can't teach without pupils, Dora. Where are they?"

"Oh, they're here. They're up beyont, in the woods. They'll come when they hear the bell." Dora climbed up on a bench and found a handbell behind a rafter in the corner. "I'll ring it for you," she said.

I stowed my dinner bucket under the bench and placed the willow switches in the corner. I was ready for my first day as a country schoolteacher. All at once I turned chilly and started shaking. I was scared.

Dora rang the bell loud and long. Suddenly, like stampeding cattle, my pupils broke forth out of the brush. In a wild rush they surged across the school yard, funnelled through the door, and arranged themselves noisily on the benches. When the dust and clatter had subsided, I made a quick inventory. Except for five boys, all were under twelve, and barefooted, and most of them were dirty and uncombed.

"Good morning, boys and girls," I said in greeting. "I'm your new teacher." I smiled brightly, I hoped, because inside I was still shaky. "My name is Priscilla Blake. You may call me Miss Blake or, if you like, you may call me Miss Prissy."

A heavy, black-browed boy in the back row leaned forward, punched a lank towhead in front of him, and whispered something. They both snickered. A Hatters boy, no doubt. I rapped on the table. "The boy who just whispered," I said, striving for dignity, "—what is your name?"

"Joe Hatters," he said smugly, and sent a mouthful of tobacco juice toward a crack in the floor but missed.

"Oh, yes, I've heard of you, Joe." I stepped down from the platform. "I hear you've run off two or three men teachers. Is that right?"

Joe spat again through his teeth. "Yeah, I reckon that's about right."

"And I also heard that you are not going to stand for any woman teacher and will run me off the first day." I pushed up my ruffled sleeves and tried to look meek and helpless, but I was not feeling meek. My momentary fright had been replaced by a calm determination to show this bully.

Joe's face turned an angry red. He looked around threateningly, then back at me. "Whoever tattled, I'll break ever' bone in their body," he said, snarling.

"But you did say it, Joe?" I asked sweetly. "You did say you were going to run me off today?"

Joe stuck out his chin. "I reckon I did, and I don't take nothin' back. Teachin' school ain't no woman's job. My pa said so."

I patted my braids and settled my neck ruffles. "Suppose you come up and get acquainted with me. You might change your mind. But before you come, Joe, get rid of that tobacco."

Joe scowled so that his heavy eyebrows came together, but he made no move to obey. "I ain't taking orders from no woman," he said, growling. A fat boy beside him laughed.

"You tell her, Joe," he whispered loudly.

I raised my eyebrows. "Why, Joe, I'm surprised. Surely you are not afraid of me?"

At that Joe stepped out into the aisle and came toward me warily. His bush of black hair stuck out like straw. He spat at the stove as he passed.

I held out my hand. "We can shake hands, anyway, can't we, before you run me off?"

Somebody giggled, and Joe's swarthy face turned beet

red, but he stuck out his hand. I laughed, for the old trick had worked. Joe was as easy as Pinky to bring to his knees. His yell made the shingles rattle.

"Now get up," I ordered, still holding Joe's arm. "And get rid of that tobacco. You are not to chew in this schoolroom again." I led him to the stove. When he had disposed of his chew, I faced him about. "Now, are you still going to run me off today, Joe?"

"No, ma'am, but please don't do that again." His face brightened. "Gee, Miss Prissy, can you show me how you done that?"

"Someday, when I think you deserve to know. But not now."

Joe went back to his seat, holding the arm I had twisted and looking at it in a puzzled manner. There was a shuffling sound at the door, and I caught sight of a pair of greenish-black coattails, attached to the living image of Ichabod Crane, disappearing through the opening. Without a doubt it was the preacher. Apparently, it was his sneaking day, and he had seen me subduing the school's worst bad boy. Such a ladylike way to open school. Mama would not have been proud of my introduction to the head trustee.

Dora raised her hand. "Preacher Higgins seen you conquer Joe," she said excitedly.

"That's fine. He should have stayed longer. Now if there are any more of you boys planning to run me off, come on up, and let's get it over."

No one made a move. The room was perfectly still. A yellow jacket zoomed in through the doorway, took a quick look around, and left hurriedly.

The rest of the day was not easy, even after conquering Joe. The children had but few books, and those they had were not much use. Some had brought old blue-backed spellers their fathers had used. Some had McGuffey readers, and a few had arithmetics, no two alike. One little boy produced a Mormon Bible, the only book his family possessed.

I had brought a map of North America, which I hung from a knot on the log wall. I assigned arithmetic problems for the older pupils to work at the board, using the few greasy stubs of chalk we could find. Another group studied from the spelling books while I tried the younger children on their alphabet and reading.

Joe Hatters, who was sixteen, could do only the simplest sums. His brother, a fat, greasy boy of fourteen called Pudge, spent his time writing words on the board which he covered with his hand and showed slyly to his neighbors, then quickly rubbed out. Zeke Hatters, a thin, sallow-faced boy of fifteen, was quick as a flash at adding and subtracting and seemed ready for long division. Zeke's pale eyes brightened when I praised him for his perfect lesson.

"You like arithmetic, don't you, Zeke?"

"Yes'm, I shore do," he said. "I know all my tables 'cept the twelves, and I woulda knowed them, but the baby got aholt of my book and tore them out."

"Zeke, you can help me with the beginners' arithmetic. Take these children to the corner there, and drill them in addition. You might be a schoolteacher yourself someday. Would you like that?"

"Yes, ma'am, I shore would." He got up, a pleased look in his eyes. As he passed Joe on the end seat, Joe ducked suddenly and butted Zeke in the stomach with his head. Zeke grunted and sat down, doubled up with pain, his face a pasty white. So these were the mean Hatters boys: a tough bully, a sickly, undernourished lad who served as a human punching bag for his brother, and a dirty, leering lout of fourteen, whispering obscenities to his schoolmates.

I poured water from the bucket over my handerkerchief and took a dipperful to Zeke. I bathed his face, and he smiled weakly and drank the water. "It's my side, ma'am. It's got a misery in it. I couldn't help it."

"Of course you couldn't." I turned to Joe. I could have

pounded him into the dirt. Such a cowardly trick! He edged
away from me, his hands behind him.

"You needn't be afraid," I said scornfully. "I wouldn't
touch such a sniveling coward. Now come up front, and
let's get this business settled. I have no time for smart
alecks in my school."

Joe made no move to come.

I walked over to the corner of the room and selected a
switch, not one that would raise "whelps" on a wildcat but
a long keen one that would sting like all get-out.

"Are you coming up here, Joe, or do you want an arm
cracked?" I asked. "You only had a sample before."

For a few seconds the room was so quiet I could hear
the drip from the leaking waterbucket on the warped
cottonwood floor. Suddenly Dora screamed. "Look out, Miss
Priss." I whirled in time to see Pudge coming over a bench
behind me, an open pocket knife in his hand. I caught his
wrist as he sprang, and I twisted it. As the knife clattered
to the floor Pudge squealed like a stuck pig.

I picked up the knife. "Get to your seat, Pudge, and if
you move one step out of it until I tell you, you will have
to crawl home tonight." I turned to Joe.

"Come here, Joe, and come in a hurry." I was not sure
what I would do if Joe came out fighting. He was taller
than I and looked tough. But Joe came.

I looked him squarely in the eyes. "Joe, you are much too
big for me to whip, but when you act like a child, you
must be punished like one."

Joe shifted from one foot to the other. His face was sullen
and his eyes hard. He clenched his fists. "I dast you to,"
he said hoarsely.

I laid the switch on his shoulders hard. I had to do it.
I had to show him and Pudge and the others that the
Hatters boys were not going to run me off or run the
school. Joe winced under the switch but stood and took it.

When I stopped, the surly look went out of his eyes, and his hands unclenched. I decided there was hope for him. Then I turned around. Preacher Higgins was sitting on the front bench, grim as a death's head. I laid down the switch and waited. He said nothing. "Well," I asked sharply, "what do you want?"

He pointed to Joe, who was rubbing his nose hard. "You —you licked that boy?" he asked.

I swallowed hard, and my eyes stung. A schoolteacher for a day! Of course, the preacher would fire me, and I would never earn enough to pay for the palomino or the clothes Mama made me. Suddenly I turned on Preacher Higgins.

"Well, what do you expect? What else could I do? If you had a decent schoolhouse, if you tried to do something to keep a teacher, these children would not be such hoodlums. Why should they want to come to such a school? What do you expect a teacher to do in a shack like this and nothing to work with—not even books for the children!"

The preacher scowled, but I was too angry to be afraid of him. "A fine trustee you are, sneaking in and out on the teachers, trying to scare them to death. Well, you don't scare me, Preacher Higgins. I—I—well, say something!"

The Adam's apple in Preacher Higgin's throat jumped up and down under his collar band. He looked as if he had seen a ghost, but he left without a word. The younger children stared, their eyes big and scared. I was ashamed that I had frightened them. I saw that my hands were shaking.

"I guess it is about time for recess," I said. "You are excused."

They went out on tiptoe. When they got outside, they broke and ran.

I had no more trouble the rest of the day. Pudge and Joe made no attempt to study but watched every move I made. When I dismissed the pupils for the day, Lissy Bates, a shy little girl, came and put her arms around me. "Miss Prissy," she whispered, "please stay and teach. Nobody ever teached us like you do. I like you."

I hugged her to me. "I'll do my best," I promised. "I like you, too."

Dora came in with an armful of leafy branches. We tied them together and made brooms. With them we brushed the worst of the mud and litter through the cracks and left the little schoolhouse open to the wind and weather and the pigs that roamed the woods for acorns.

I wanted to stay in the shabby little barn of a schoolhouse that had only crumbs of chalk. The children seemed eager to learn and had had such little opportunity. Even most of the older ones could be taught self-respect along with their multiplication tables and spelling lessons. My head began to seethe with plans, but I came back to the gloomy conclusion that I had practically ordered Preacher Higgins out of the schoolroom, and so I would be ordered out next.

I told the Carters about my day as we ate supper. "I don't think I will be here long," I said. "I don't know what I will do with all my clothes, and I was looking forward to riding Daisy some more."

Page listened without comment. When he finished, he pushed back his chair. "Hetty, I have some business across the pasture. I may not be back by bedtime." With that, he saddled his horse and rode off.

Chapter 10

When Dora and I arrived at school the next morning, the door was closed. I opened it gingerly, expecting it to fall, but strangely, it held.

"It growed hinges in the night," Dora commented sagely.

It had indeed grown hinges, and the hinges were nailed on firmly with shiny new nails. I looked around to see if other miracles had taken place. They had. The floor had been scrubbed, scrubbed so hard that soft little splinters stuck up all over it like bristles on a hog's back. It was still damp in spots and smelled of wet wood and lye soap. Even my table was noticeably cleaner.

"Miss Prissy," Dora squealed, "looky, it's chalk—new chalk!" And there on the chalk tray were six long sticks of gleaming white chalk. Someone had certainly waved a magic wand.

I knew Page Carter's mysterious "business" after supper the night before must have been with the preacher, but

how he managed to get the floor scrubbed and to get new
hinges, and even the new chalk, was beyond my knowing.
But it was encouraging, and another day's pay would mean
another dollar for a stirrup, even if there never was a
filly to wear it.

Dora rang the bell, and the children came running out of
the brush, not stampeding this time, followed leisurely by
the Hatters boys and Speck and Skeet Jenks, the stutter-
ing twins from Turkey Hollow. At the edge of the school-
yard, the twins carefully ejected chews of tobacco and
wiped their feet on the stubby grass.

I waited in the doorway, the dignified teacher Mama
would be proud of. No more tomboy tricks today or ever
again. I would be stern but kind, come what may. If I
could teach the week out before the preacher discharged me,
I would do the best I possibly could. If I had to leave tomorrow, I would have done my best today.

I had dropped off to sleep the night before, planning
great things for my pupils. Give me time enough, and my
school would have the eyes of the nation on it—or maybe
the whole world. I would tell the children stories of the
world's great leaders and inspire them to become Alexan-
ders or Napoleons. Perhaps I would go down in history as
one of the great teachers, to be remembered with Socrates,
Pliny, and others—that is, if Preacher Higgins would mind
his own business and leave me alone.

Filled with noble thoughts and an overwhelming desire
to stick my foot out and trip Preacher Higgins next time
I saw him sneaking into the classroom, I lined the children
up before the door.

"Good morning." I greeted them cheerfully. "March
quietly into the room, and take your seats. Then we will
get down to the business of learning. I have come here to
teach you, not to fight you. If you want to learn, I will
help you all I can. If you just want to spend your time
making mischief, you might as well turn around and

march home, because that is where you are going the first time you cause trouble."

I stood aside. The pupils filed in, eyeing me warily. There was not a whisper, even from the smallest one. The only sounds were the shuffling of bare feet on the damp cottonwood floor and the clatter of tin dinner-buckets being lined up along the wall. It had actually worked. My dignified manner had impressed them.

Full of enthusiasm, I waited for them to settle down. "Pudge, I want you to come and sit just back of the recitation bench. You can study better away from the other boys."

Pudge, sitting next to Joe, turned to him with a sly grin, nudged him, and winked. Joe scowled.

"Did you hear me, Pudge? Take this seat in front, please."

Pudge glared at me, his heavy-lidded eyes malevolent as a snapping turtle's. "I ain't agoin' to do it," he said, snarling. "I don't have to mind you. My pa said so. Pa said I don't have to take orders from no upstart woman in flipperty skirts, and if you hurt me again he'll have the law on you." Pudge looked around, proud of his bravado.

The room was still. The Jenks twins were absorbed in watching a yellow jacket cleaning his feet on the window sill. Zeke was hard at work writing figures on a slate.

"So you told your pa on me," I said. "Pudge, I don't think I have ever seen a worse coward. All right then, sit there until I tell you to move. Let the others see the brave Hatters boy who is afraid of his teacher and tells his pa on her. But—when I say move, Pudge, you had better move."

I stepped to the corner of the room and took one of the switches that Dora said would raise "whelps" on a wildcat, but I was sure I would not have to use it. I knew a coward when I saw one, but I had had enough of Pudge's impertinence, and if it took "whelps" to tame him, he should have them.

"I'm ready, Pudge; come here!"

Pudge looked at Joe, his grimy dark face sulky. But Joe stared straight ahead.

"Git her, Joe," Pudge whimpered. "Don't let her lick me."

I settled my pins in my braids and folded my arms. "All right, Pudge, move!"

Pudge moved closer to Joe and whispered something. Suddenly Joe caught him and shoved him into the aisle. "Here," he said hoarsely, "he's jest itchin' for a lickin', Miss Priss. Give him a good un. He durn shore needs it."

"I took Pudge's arm, led him up front, and turned him around. The surly look on his face was the scared hatred of a coward. His hands and face were dirty, and his clothes were dirty. His big bare feet were rusty as the ground.

"All right, Pudge," I said sternly, "what have you to say for yourself?"

"I won't do it no more," Pudge whimpered. "Don't lick me; please, don't lick me."

"Now, aren't you the brave one?" I said, shaming him. "Crying before I even touch you. A big boy like you, almost old enough to shave."

There was a sharp rap at the open door, and I looked up. The rap was made with the heavy handle of a quirt, the kind of lash used on balky horses and mules. Another visitor, but not the preacher this time. The latest was undoubtedly the villain of the piece. He had the rough black beard, the shifty black eyes, and the yellow buck teeth that villains in a play are supposed to have. His dirty clothes and greasy black-felt hat, even the black scuffed boots, fitted the part. I wanted to clap, his entrance was so well timed. There I was, switch in hand, Pudge squalling like a beaten thing, and Pudge's pa—for it was he—takes his cue and comes on stage in the nick of time to save his errant son. It was too funny.

"Go on," I said encouragingly. "Speak your piece; it's your turn."

Blackbeard blinked and gulped and aimed a mouthful of tobacco at a weed beside the door. Then his lines came to him. "I ain't goin' to have you beatin' my boys. You got to stop it."

"Is that all?" I asked.

Pa Hatters' eyes flashed. "No woman is gonna lick my boys," he snarled, swinging his loaded quirt. "Jest you dare touch one of 'em another lick, and I'll——" He raised his quirt threateningly.

"You'll do what, you big brave man, who has to bring along a leather quirt to protect himself from an upstart woman teacher with flipperty skirts? Scared, too, aren't you? Tell me, what makes you and your two boys such cowards?"

The man took a step toward me. "No woman ain't goin' to—" he said, sputtering, and glared at me.

I glared right back. "Oh, yes, she is." I shook my finger under his nose. "A woman is giving you orders right now. Get out of my schoolroom. Get out and stay out until you can come back like a man and not a coward."

He picked at the leather thongs of the quirt. "You beat Pudge thar. I ain't goin' to have it."

"I have not even touched Pudge with a switch. Look at him, crying because he is a coward, scared of this switch." I held it up.

Pa Hatters backed away a step and held his arm in front of his face.

"Come on, Pudge," he said, blustering. "You don't have to stay here and be mistreated."

Pudge had stopped crying. He was standing in the middle of the floor, twisting his big bare toes through a crack in the floor. I waited, but he said nothing.

"All right, Pudge, go ahead if you do not expect to behave here. But don't come back if you do."

"Come on, Pudge," his father bellowed. "Get going."

Pudge looked down at his toes. "I aim to stay," he said defiantly.

I turned to his father. "He may stay, but I am telling him and I am telling you that if your boys come to school, they will behave or be punished. The government is paying me good money to teach here, and I have wasted most of two days trying to do something you should have done yourself. Now go."

Pa Hatters left, muttering darkly through his buck teeth and slapping his boots with the leather quirt. Pudge was still boring at the crack with his toes, a shamefaced look on his dirty face. I went to the corner, untied a flour sack I had brought, and took out a washpan, soap, and a towel. I handed them to Pudge.

"I want to see what you look like clean. Get water from the bucket, and go outside and scrub your face and hands. Take this comb, and get the burrs out of your hair. And when you come to school tomorrow, your feet had better be clean. Heat a tubful of water, get in it, and soak."

The children shuffled uneasily in their seats and tried to hide their bare feet. "All of you try it," I said. "Water won't hurt any of you."

Dora giggled. "That's what my mammy says. She says folks around here must think water's pizen."

I hardly knew the boy who came in a little later. Pudge's face was so clean it shone. Someday he might even learn to wash his ears, but now the clean face and hands helped. I hardly knew the towel either. Pudge grinned sheepishly. "Ma'll wash it, and I can bring it back tomorrow," he said. "I never dried on nothing like that before."

Chapter 11

The week went by, and not a word from the preacher. Even Dora was puzzled. "Pappy said he reckoned the old buzzard must be up to something," she said gloomily. "They're all joshing Joe Hatters about you, Miss Priss. He made his pa cut his hair, and now he's rarin' for shoes."

"But the Hatters boys haven't been here since Tuesday," I said. "I thought they had quit."

"No'm, they didn't quit." Dora grinned at me. "You shore got that Hatters bunch buffaloed, Miss Priss. Old Buck told it around that if you'd been a man, you'da whupped him. He's afeared of you."

"Not that man, Dora." I remembered the thick, hard muscles of his arms. "He could whip me with one hand tied behind him. But I hope the boys come back, especially Zeke. That boy's smart."

"Yes'm, he's not like the rest." Dora plodded on, her eyes shining with fun. "They're gettin' their cotton out now.

Buck Hatters never had a patch bigger'n you could spit
over and most always lets that rot in the field. But Joe's
bound to have shoes, and Pappy said dog if he didn't have
the whole outfit picking. They'll be back."

A broom made its appearance in the schoolroom Wednesday morning, and Dora and I stayed and swept out when
school was dismissed for the day. The little girls begged to
help, so we took turns sweeping and dusting and straighten-
ing the benches. The scrubbed floor was easy to sweep, as
the dirt went right through the cracks.

After Tuesday only the small children had come to
school. The cotton, dried out from Sunday night's rain, had
to be picked, and the older boys stayed out to help.

"Cotton's not much good this year," Dora told me. "Wee-
vils been thick as mustard. 'Twon't take long to pick what's
left. Miss Prissy, I sure hope you stay. Pappy said it all
depends on the preacher, and once he gets his head set, you
couldn't budge him with a cow pen full of billygoats."

The week had been pleasant enough. Hetty had warned
me to look out for a visit from the trustees on Friday.
They might not come, of course, but Fridays were visiting
days for anyone who wanted to come.

The expected visit of the trustees weighed on my mind,
but I determined to make the best of it. For the first time,
and likely the last, the trustees would see what a lady they
had hired. I would wear the blue-and-green plaid skirt,
Mama's favorite, with a white shirtwaist. I even considered
wearing the sailor hat with the broody mallard but decided
against it. After all, there was no use carrying things too
far. But I did take out my two best flounced petticoats. If
anything could save the day, the petticoats would.

Hetty caught me on Thursday night practicing a haughty
freezing stare before my folding bed mirror. I threw my
head back, and holding my skirts tightly around my ankles,
acknowledged an introduction to the trustees sweetly and

graciously, as Mama would do. They would literally be
swept off their feet by my queenly grace. I must make an
especially good impression on the preacher. Everything,
Dora's pappy said, depended on him.

"Well, well," Hetty said, chuckling. "If that doesn't fix
them, nothing will." She settled down comfortably in the
rocking chair. "Reckon they've never seen such a fancy outfit. Women folks around here just wear cotton checks."

My dress was long and full. My new black-kid shoes were
high and laced closely. Under no circumstances would anyone see even a small bit of my black stockings. But in spite
of my plans, I had an uneasy feeling as I dropped off to
sleep.

Friday afternoon was an occasion—like church on Sunday
meeting day, Dora told me. It was called literary society,
and there were speeches, songs, and spelling matches. Everyone who could would be on hand.

The day was bright with the late September sunshine
and was lazily warm. I took my dinner bucket and went
with the little girls to the grapevine swing beside the
creek. After we had eaten our lunches, I sat on the grassy
bank, watching the children play. A wild grapevine thick
as my wrist hung from a tall pecan tree, and the children
took turns swinging out over the steep bank of the dry
creek.

Dora and Lissy Bates and Josie Evans were close beside
me. I never got far from these three. Josie was telling
about the new doctor who had come to take up practice.
"Pappy said he were duded up like a parlor lamp. He wears
city clothes and parts his hair in the middle."

"Oh, Miss Prissy," Dora said, squealing, "why don't you
set your cap for the doctor and marry him? Then you can
stay here even if the preacher runs you off."

"But I don't want to set my cap for anybody. I don't
want to marry. All I want is a horse and saddle."

"But you have to marry sometimes, Miss Prissy," Dora insisted. "Everybody marries and has young uns."

Lissy caught my hand and squeezed it hard. "Don't marry the doctor and have young uns," she said tensely. "Stay here and teach this school."

"No, I won't marry him, and I'll stay if the preacher will let me, but what I want now is to swing on that grapevine."

I jumped up and caught the grapevine and ran back as far as I could, then swung out for the long glide over the creek bank. Too late, I saw Preacher Higgins. As usual, he had bobbed up out of thin air right in my path. We collided and rolled down the steep bank together.

I landed head down, my feet against the bank, the beautiful ruffled petticoats I had worn especially for the preacher draped like Monday's wash over the wild briars. Preacher Higgins landed on his feet above me and stared at me mournfully, his straggly little black beard wagging protestingly. I struggled for a dignified attitude, attempting the haughty freezing stare I had planned to assume in greeting him. I almost choked. One of my laced shoes pointed toward the North Star, and the other was caught in a protruding root that would not let go.

The little girls lined up along the bank like crows on a limb to see what had happened except for Dora, who scrambled down the bank to help me. She landed in front of the preacher like a whirlwind, all mixed up with dust and leaves.

"Now don't you dast say one word to Miss Prissy," she said, exploding. "And don't go around saying she's no lady. Miss Prissy is the nicest lady you ever saw, and you know it." She stood before me, her skinny little arms spread-eagled as if she were afraid the preacher would grab me and beat me. "Now you quit sneaking up on Miss Prissy. She whupped the Hatters boys, and she can whup you."

The preacher turned and fled into the brush. Dora unhooked my petticoats from the briars and my foot from the root and helped me up. I was weak from laughing. I knew that as a teacher at Oak Grove my hours were numbered, but the sight of the preacher's face, as he had stood there above me, was almost worth it.

"Dora, I am just no lady," I said, wiping my eyes. "I might as well go home right now and pack my trunk. I am finished as a teacher at Oak Grove."

She brushed the leaves from my clothes and hair. "Don't you worry about that preacher, Miss Prissy," she said consolingly. "My pappy will see to him. Pappy said when the time came, he would step in and have his say."

I hated the thought of not getting the palomino filly, but at seventeen I could not worry much. I flirted my skirts back and forth as we went to the schoolhouse. "Well, I wore starched petticoats just on the preacher's account," I said pertly, "and he certainly got a good look at them. I hope he liked them, for it's the last time I'll ever wear them."

"He liked 'em, all right," Josie Evans assured me mournfully. "He were goggled-eyed as a toad. I'd shore hate for my pa to know it, Miss Prissy, but your stockings showed clean to your knees. Pa's a sight about women's stockings showin'."

I giggled. Pa was certainly going to get an eyeful if I stayed. I was through with long skirts. "You won't tell him, will you?" I asked.

"He's apt to ast me." Josie sighed. "He ginerally do, and I'd not say no."

By the middle of the afternoon my visitors began drifting in. Several of the girls sat down on a bench at the back. They wore dresses of colored calico, with starched ruffled sunbonnets perched on their stiff pompadours. Once seated, they removed their bonnets and dabbed their heavily powdered faces with their bonnet strings.

The girls sat stiffly and self-consciously as a group of

lanky half-grown boys took their places on a bench oppo-
site. The boys wore the heavy, coarse shoes that marked
them as adults. Their long tight pants were pulled high
over faded shirts and were held up by brightly colored suspenders. Tired-looking stooped women in dark calico wrap-
pers and slatted sunbonnets came in twos and threes with
young children hanging to their skirts. Some had babies in
their arms. The women slipped silently into the room and
found seats in front of the girls. They had walked miles to
hear the songs, the speeches, and the spelling match.

I welcomed the visitors and said I hoped they would enjoy the program. Then I asked for volunteers—anyone who
would sing, speak, or do anything—as Dora had told me
that was what I should do. For several minutes there was
not a word from or a move by anyone. Then a long slim
boy with pale hair and eyes got up and came forward,
looking at the floor.

"Will you tell us your name and what you will do?" I
asked.

He stepped over to the stove to inter his juicy tobacco
chew in the ashes; then, hitching up his tight pants, without a word or look in my direction, he sang. There were
eight or ten stanzas of the mournful ditty, and he sang
them all in a thin, high, nasal voice. When he had finished
burying his cowboy on the lone prairee, he stopped for
breath.

The audience clapped long and loud. The singer waited
for the clapping to stop and then encored with an old ballad I had not heard before. I asked him to sing it again.
The words of the first stanza were:

> As I went down the new-cut road
> I met the possum and the toad;
> The possum cut the pigeon wing,
> The toad began to whistle and sing.

As his thin tenor voice dramatized the ballad I thought of my time at Oak Grove school and how much had happened. I too had gone down the new-cut road. There had surely been possums and toads, but what was ahead?

My reverie was interrupted by the trustees descending upon us. As they came in I smoothed down my skirt, relieved that for once the preacher could see me at my best. He led the way, followed by a red-faced short man and a thin oldish one with a drooping sandy moustache. They were Aaron Akers and Sandy Goff. Hetty had described them well. They did not so much as glance in my direction but moved in a body to the recitation bench. I said, "Good afternoon, gentlemen," but they remained silent and aloof. They neither smiled nor frowned. When the spelling match was over, they left.

I was far from easy in my mind about their visit, but there was nothing I could do, so I went ahead with the program. One of my little boys, Cephas Ladd, pushed on by his seatmate, Bud Ives, got up and danced a hoedown on the splintery cottonwood floor to the music of Bud's twanging Jew's harp. Cephas was like a monkey jiggling on a string. His spindly arms and legs flung in and out, but his sharp little face was set and unsmiling as it always was. Did he never smile, I wondered? Was life so hard that even pleasure must be taken with a grim, set face? I vowed to do something for these people: the old-young women with tired faces and the children who could not laugh. If I could stay, I would at least teach them to laugh.

I dismissed school and told the visitors I was glad they had come and would they come again? They answered politely. Yes, ma'am, they enjoyed the program, and yes, ma'am, they would come again.

I picked up the broom and banged it against the door. "Is it always like this?" I asked, my fighting mood back again.

"Yes'm, 'cept when it rains," Dora answered cheerfully. "Then the women can't come."

The Carter house looked good to me that night. I had taught school for a whole week and had not been fired yet. Whatever came, I would have two whole days—no trustees, no fights, and a horse to ride. I set my dinner bucket on the kitchen table and let out a fair imitation of one of Pinky's warwhoops.

"Two days of freedom from corsets and petticoats! Two days to ride the chestnut mare!" I fairly shouted.

Hetty was rolling out cooky dough, and the warm kitchen was spicy with baking odors. "Page wants you to help him run in a heifer to take to town tomorrow. But help yourself to cookies. You'll be hungry before we eat."

Page called from the lot. "Your horse is ready, Priss. Get your pants on."

Hetty's gold-toothed smile flashed. "Now if that's not just like Page. But don't let him vex you, Prissy."

"Not me, Hetty."

I tore out across the porch to my room, my mouth and hands full of hot, crumbly cookies. I was out of the plaid skirt and shirtwaist in no time. Punk Willard's jeans, fresh from the iron, hung over my rocking chair. Good old Punk.

"Whoopee! I'm coming, Page," I yelled, as I climbed the rail fence of the corral.

Chapter 12

The first thing I knew it was middle October. Frost had yellowed the grass and leaves, and I was still teaching at Oak Grove School. Soon I would have my first paycheck. The preacher had not shown his face since that fateful day of the grapevine swing, but new glass in the windows gave evidence of someone's interest in the little log schoolhouse. We were glassed in for the winter.

Walking the woods road was a pleasant interlude during school days. The red sumac bushes glowed like brush fires along the fringes of the woods and in the fence rows. The post-oak and blackjack timber, never so daring as sumac, changed slowly into less flamboyant colors of dull gold and mahogany with an occasional splash of scarlet where a haw tree had crept in. Frost nipped the yellow persimmons hidden away in the woods and left them as pinkish sugary balls on the bare tree-limbs. Our walks home from school were broken into a series of forays off the road

for the autumn fruit. The shortening days were bright
with mellow sunshine, as the fall rains were late in starting.

The frost must surely have nipped the bare toes of the
schoolchildren, for the only shoes in sight were Joe's coarse
new brogans. These he brought to school, tied together and
hung over his shoulders, and wore only in the schoolroom,
clumping about awkwardly and shedding them with obvious
relief as soon as he was outside the school yard. In the
stiff, cheap shoes Joe lost the wild animal grace of movement that barefooted he possessed. The uncomfortable half-
limp disturbed me, but I said nothing. It was endured, I
knew, for a stubborn bit of pride some long-forgotten an-
cestor had bequeathed to him. His wearing the shoes was
a sort of tribute, and I was secretly pleased. Joe, at
least, had accepted me as a lady, and I was glad of that
bit of pride in him.

I asked Dora why the children went barefooted these
frosty mornings when they should be wearing shoes.

"They're used to it, Miss Priss. Our feet's tough as whit-
leather. Anyway," she added shrewdly, "it warms up by
dinner, and we forget by then it's been cold."

The youngsters had good stuff in them, I knew. Just give
them a chance, and they would do things anyone would
be proud of; especially Dora, for she had a good mind.

"You know what?" Dora said excitedly. "My pappy 'lowed
he'll have enough left when rent's paid and grub's bought
for the winter to buy Mammy and me new shoes."

"Oh, my goodness, how nice."

"Yes'm, it shore is. Mammy told him he needed shoes
worser'n her, for sometimes he's ailin' in the winter. He's
out in the weather most, and his feet are near on the
ground now. But Pappy said all he needed were new soles
to hold him another winter. Mammy said they'd do well to
hold him till Christmas, but Pappy said they'd have to. It
was women and children first with him if he had to go
down with the ship. Don't he beat all?"

"Your pappy is a good man, Dora." It was plain she was fond of her pappy.

"No'm." She shook her head. "He ain't good. He swears something fearful and teases Mammy a sight, but he says he reckons he'll do in a pinch. It makes Mammy mad as fury 'cause he won't spend a cent on hisself. He says he ain't worth it."

"I am glad you will have new shoes, Dora. You don't get new ones often, do you?"

"Miss Prissy, in two winters I ain't had good-enough shoes to go to school. But Pappy says somebody in the family orta have book learnin', and if it takes shoes on my feet for me to learn somethin' in my head, he could wrop his uns in towsacks."

I had not yet met Dora's pappy, but my heart warmed to him. He had the right spirit, the kind that helped the Pilgrims. I had been thinking of buying shoes for Dora out of my first check if she did not start wearing them soon. She shivered mornings in her thin checked-cotton dresses. She had two, she told me proudly: one to wear and one to wash. She was wearing both now for warmth and was always clean, but she would need warmer clothes when the fall northers came. Page had said Dora's pappy was not able to work a big crop and never had much money to spare.

"You will have to have a new dress to wear with those new shoes," I said. "A warm winter one."

"No'm, Pappy said he was afeared not. He's got to lay up flour and sugar and coffee for winter, and that'll take all his money after the rent's paid. I'll be satisfied to get shoes, Miss Prissy. But Mammy's making me a coat out of her weddin' dress—brown alpacy. It's sure pretty and fine as catgut for me. Mammy said it was a mite thin for a coat, but by the time she lined it with outin' flannel and her black underskirt, it'll keep me warm as a bug in a rug." Dora laughed happily. "New shoes and new coat.

Goodness, Miss Priss, I'll be rigged out 'most as fine as you."

That hurt. I had hated my fancy new clothes all along. After the grapevine-swing affair I declared I would not wear petticoats and long dresses again, but when the preacher sent word I could teach the month out, I decided I had better be on my good behavior. But seeing Dora and the other children come barefooted on frosty mornings wearing the same thin clothes they had worn in September made me feel guilty and ashamed.

Letters came every week from Mama. Pinky wanted to come and stay with me. He said I could teach him all the grammar he needed and keep him up with his lessons, and he could ride Daisy after school. Mama wanted to know if I used buttermilk and meal on my face and hands at night and if I had worn the red gloves.

Papa added a note that he would see Joe Edwards about the filly the next trip he made to the Choctaw country, but remember what he had said about men and horses: keep a firm grip on the reins and never lose my head even if I lost my hat.

Doc wrote that he could just see me taking on Pudge's pa for a round, and he would not take ten dollars for my story about the grapevine swing. He had told Dozie and Jeb about it, and they had laughed the rest of the day.

Mr. Brending sent me erasers, a box of chalk, and some charts he hoped I could use. The Lynwood school board, thank the lord, had voted money to replace the old out-of-date charts that had hung on the school walls from time immemorial, and I could use the old ones to teach the children about the human body, which so far had not gone out of date.

I could hardly wait for Monday to hang up the charts and show them to the children. One showed the complete skeleton, one the organs of the body, another the circulatory and nervous systems, and the last the body's bright red muscular covering. Hetty looked them over carefully with great interest.

"Land of merciful goodness," she said, marveling. "I never knew I had all that in me. No wonder we have so many aches and pains."

I hung the charts on the log wall. The children were fascinated, their eyes big with wonder and curiosity. When they were not reciting, the children could do little but gaze at the charts. I explained the bone structure and they learned some of the bones by name. That was easy enough, but the chart on which the stomach and abdominal organs were illustrated and those of the red muscles and circulatory system seemed to embarrass them. They would neither ask nor answer questions about them.

On Tuesday I had two unexpected visitors. Shortly after the noon recess two men I had not seen before dropped in. With a brief "Howdy, Ma'am," they seated themselves on the end of the recitation bench and stared at the charts open-mouthed. They wore the usual faded, patched jean pants and coarse, worn shoes. Their unshaven faces had the hard, dried-up look that I had come to associate with the men of the region. It was not considered polite to ask visitors their business, so I ignored their presence and went on with my arithmetic class. Soon the men got up, slapped their shapeless black-felt hats on their heads, and left. I thought no more of the incident except to note that it was my first visit from male parents.

On Wednesday two more men dropped in, said "Howdy, Ma'am," stared at the charts for a few minutes, and left. Dora spoke to me about it at recess.

"Them men were Mart Ebberts and Joe Hobbs from over

at Dobson's Corner. They must be up to something, Miss Prissy. They never come to school before."

"Well, I am glad they came. They seemed to like our new charts."

"No'm, I don't think they did. They ain't the kind to take to new learnin'," Dora said gloomily. "I'm afraid they're up to something."

Soon after noon on Friday the usual visitors arrived—the girls in their stiffly starched dresses and sunbonnets, the lanky grown-up boys in drab work clothes highlighted by new rainbow-colored suspenders, and the mothers leading or carrying small children. For the first time, men came—six or eight of them. Crops had been gathered, and they had free time on their hands. They waited outside until the women and young folks were seated, then crowded together on the narrow recitation bench. Two or three had even shaved for the occasion, and their still-wet hair was combed flatly over their white foreheads. Mournful-eyed Sandy Goff, the trustee, was there, his droopy colorless moustache arching over the darker stubble of his chin. He, like the rest, appeared to be hypnotized by the charts on the wall. Unquestionably, the charts had made an impression.

After recess the visitors rearranged themselves. Two of the visiting boys moved over to sit beside girls. This, Dora told me later, was a sign they were promised. Romance was as simple as that.

When everyone was settled, a hush of expectancy replaced the shuffling and whispering. Then through the door strode the slim singer of cowboy ballads. This time he wore shining high-heeled boots, the tops stitched in a fancy pattern of red and white. When he had seated himself and removed his hat, his small round head towered nakedly above those beside him. His straight colorless locks had been shorn high

above his ears, leaving only a cap of short hair perched on
the white border of his skull. His blue shirt and coarse pants
were as store new as his boots.

Togged out in his new finery, the young singer quite
obviously had come to school with courting in mind. I wondered who was the object of his affections. A plump dark-
eyed girl was openly shining her eyes in his direction. She
moved over on the bench invitingly, crowding the girls
next to her, but the singer did not look in her direction.

When sober little Cephas Ladd finished his hoedown and
Bud Ives put away his harmonica, the clapping ceased.
Then the young ballad singer stood up. As he came forward
with a slight swagger to his thin shoulders, he disposed of
his chew neatly in the ashes of the stove. With a jerky
little bow in my direction, he turned around and sang, but
not a cowboy ballad. The song was a sad one about "I
loved my love and she went away," that seemed to wring
his listeners' hearts. The plump black-haired girl sniffed
audibly. I wanted to pat the boy on the shoulder and say,
"Don't take it so hard, son; there are others."

He waited patiently through the applause to sing his
encore. This number told more about his love. "Her hair
was soft as the nesting dove, her eyes like the morning sky."
At the end of each stanza the boy's thin voice trailed off
into a sad falsetto note that sent a shiver down my spine.
When he finished the song, he bowed to me again and sat
down.

When all the visitors had gone, Dora and I swept the floor
hurriedly.

"Let's hurry, Dora; I am hungry enough to eat a wolf."

"Miss Prissy"—Dora looked at me mischievously—"that
Jim Iders sure has took a shine to you."

"Jim Iders?" My mind was on the good supper Hetty
would have for me. "Who is Jim Iders, and why should he
take a shine to me?"

Dora giggled. "You know—Jim were the singing boy. He sang them songs to you, Miss Prissy, sure as shootin'! Didn't you see him bowin' to you?"

I swung at Dora with the broom. "He was not. He was singing to the black-haired girl." But Dora had skipped out the door and was waiting, grinning impishly.

I put the broom away and took my dinner bucket and books. As I closed the door Jim Iders stepped from the corner of the schoolhouse. "I'll tote your dinner bucket," he said shyly. "I aim to walk your way."

Dora skipped ahead, singing loudly, "I loved my love and she went away." I wanted to shake her when she would turn and look, then giggle and run ahead. Jim, true to his word, "toted" my dinner bucket home, or at least to the lane that led to the house. If there were anything on his mind, I never knew, because his only answers to my attempts at conversation were "Yes, ma'am," and "No, ma'am." At the end of the lane he said goodbye and swaggered off down the road, a happy smile on his face.

Dora went to the house with me. "See, I told you, and you wouldn't believe me. Next thing after he starts walking you home, he'll ask you to marry him. Watch out, Miss Prissy; you'll be promised to Jim Iders 'fore you know it."

We ran a race the rest of the way. It was Friday and cookie day. Dora's skinny legs carried her over the ground like a jackrabbit, and she was in the house, drinking milk and eating cookies, by the time I got there. She was telling Hetty about Jim's "shine" on me.

"Don't you think your ma had better start a promise box right away?" Hetty asked me, winking at Dora.

"I'm afeared so." Dora gulped as she swallowed her milk. "Pappy said Jim shore had marrying on his mind."

Chapter 13

"*We're sure going to have a spell of weather,*" Page announced Saturday afternoon. "I have to ride over to Stagg's Prairie after dinner. You can come along on Daisy if you want."

"I do have to pick up a book at the school," I answered, "so I will ride that far with you."

We took a shortcut through the woods, which seemed to drowse in the thin autumn sunlight. The birds were gone, but now and then a cricket rasped away or a bobwhite whistled mournfully. There was a feeling of waiting or slowing up for winter to come. Page rode on as I turned toward the schoolhouse. As I came near I was surprized to see the door open and about a dozen men inside. Preacher Higgins sat at the table, his face set in grim lines. Sandy Goff stood beside him, talking rapidly. When he saw me, his mouth snapped shut, and his pale eyes shifted uneasily.

I knew, as I stood there at the door, exactly how Daniel must have felt when he faced the lions. The faces turned toward me were grim and harshly accusing. My throat seemed to close up, and my legs were shaky.

"Miss Blake," Preacher Higgins said sternly, "I am right glad you came. We were aimin' to wait on you at Carter's, but it's just as well you are here. It's them pictures. Sandy says they're obs—obskeen."

I had a queer mixture of feelings. I wanted to fight, but I would be glad to be going home—because, of course, I would be. But when I thought of Dora and Zeke and even Pudge and Joe, I wanted to cry. Such mixed-up country, but I still wanted to stay in it. I wanted to do something for them and felt I might be able to do so, given a little time.

Sandy pointed an accusing finger at me. "Thar she is. Let her tell it."

And there I was in Punk Willard's jeans, Page's old jacket, and a rusty black hat before my school board and most of the men in the district. Daniel's lions could not have surveyed the scene more avidly than they. All except one. At the back of the room was a youngish-looking man, thin as a rail and the spit image of Dora. It had to be her pappy. He gave me a friendly wink, and immediately I felt better. He, at least, was on my side. Suddenly the whole affair seemed funny: the shabby, dirty little schoolhouse, the shabby, dirty men sitting there in judgment upon me. I almost burst out laughing.

"Sorry, gentlemen, I just came for a book. I'll get it and go, and you can go on with your meeting."

"Make her stay," Sandy demanded hoarsely. "Make her tell it. She can't deny it."

Preacher Higgins gave me a sorrowful look, then glared at Sandy.

"Sandy, I ain't askin' you what to do. Keep your tongue

till you're called on. Miss Blake, you been charged with bringin' obskeen—them things thar"—he pointed to the charts—"into this school. Sandy says they ain't fitten to be set before innocent children."

A hard-featured, shifty-eyed man stood up. "Look at her, wearin' pants," he sneered. "No shame to her atall. Brazen as they come, riding around astraddle like a man, too. I ain't wantin' any female wearin' pants teachin' my children."

The preacher's face took on a look of utter sadness. "Hack Mifford," he said, "as long as your children have no better than you and your old woman for a ma and a pa, the Lord have mercy on them. Any teachin' atall is better'n what you give them. Now set, Hack, and remember I'm runnin' this school."

Hack subsided, red-faced and muttering to himself.

The room was silent except for shuffling of shoes on the rough floor. The sun had dropped behind the trees, and the room had grown chill. A lanky hound dog wormed out from under a bench and stood stretching, his eyes searching the group.

The preacher's brittle voice broke the silence. "All right, Sandy, you tell her about the pitchers. Tell her what you said to me."

Sandy stood up, a little disconcerted. "Well, I say it's a shame and a disgrace to have them things there where people can see 'em. The sight of 'em gives me the cold shudders."

I giggled, remembering Friday afternoon. "You didn't shudder one cold shudder yesterday, Mr. Goff, and you looked at them the whole time you were here. You even seemed to enjoy looking at them."

A titter went around the room. Sandy glared. "I got my duty to do," he said sulkily. "I'm a trustee. I had to get evidence to testify. Them things"—he pointed to the charts, his voice rising—"them things has got no place in the schoolroom. Things like them hangs in saloons."

"You orta know about that, Sandy," the preacher said acidly. "Anything else?"

"I reckon not," Sandy stammered. "I reckon not, 'cept that they jest ain't fitten."

"Why?" I asked, and I was hopping mad. "Tell me why it is not fitting to learn how our bodies are made. The Lord made us, didn't he? Is there anything wrong in knowing how he put us together? Is there anything wrong in teaching children that they have hearts and stomachs and livers? How can it be wrong for them to know that food is digested and blood circulates through the body?" I glared at him. "Let me tell you, Sandy Goff and Hack Mifford and the rest of you, Preacher Higgins is right. The worst thing that ever happened to your children is having you for parents."

At the back of the room Dora's pappy was shaking with silent laughter. I picked up the book I had come to get. "That's all. I don't want your school any longer. I would not have stayed this long if it had not been for your children needing schooling so much and—" I had to blink hard to keep the tears back when I thought of the filly Joe Edwards was breaking for me and I would now never have. I ran out the door, and caught up the reins, and in a moment Daisy and I were headed for home at a hard run.

When I turned into the lane, I saw a paint pony tied at the gate but was too deep in my gloom to notice it was the same one that Zade and I had raced down Main Street on parade day and the same one that had practically climbed the hill to Doc's house on his two hind legs, trying every step of the way to buck me off. But, of course, it was Richard Harper, camped on the Carter doorstep with all the Carter dogs piled around him. Old Wolf, the one I would not dare to touch, had his head on Rick's knee, being scratched like a puppy.

Rick shot off the steps and came over the fence in a wild leap, whooping like a lost banshee. "She comes, she comes, madcap Prissy, the tank-town tomboy, the pulchritudinous pedagogue of Oak Grove Academy!"

I pulled Daisy up short to keep from riding him down. "What are you doing here?" I asked.

"Ah, that's my Priss," Richard said, "always the cordial welcome. It makes the long and tedious journey just to see you worthwhile. But then I knew you were just awearing for me." He slapped Daisy's flank and laughed when she waltzed sideways. "Dad's making a campaign speech at Blue Springs tonight, and I ducked out. He'll be jealous when he finds out where I have been. He likes you."

"I thought you were at the university at Norman."

"So I have been, right up to my neck. But when I heard Dad was swinging through here on his last trip, I begged to come with him. Darn it, Priss, can't you be even a little glad to see me?"

Rick was holding Daisy's bridle. He was obviously fresh from the barbershop. His dark hair, parted in the middle, arched at the corners of his forehead. His dark suit and light tan vest were new and expensive-looking, and his high starched collar was fresh from his collar box. He was, indeed, a well-dressed young man, and I knew too well what I looked like.

"You're certainly duded up like a parlor lamp," I said, borrowing a phrase from Josie Evans. "But if you want that new derby to stay new, you had better get it before Wolf eats it."

"Let him. Darn it, Priss, I can't get you off my mind— the way you looked at the parade. You were pretty as a picture. I just——"

I kicked Daisy in the flank. Surprised at such treatment, she bolted for the lot. In an instant Rick was following on his horse. We unsaddled without another word, and while

Rick pulled hay down from the loft, I ran for the house.

I was tired and dirty and in a bad humor. Dressed-up Richard Harper was the last person I wanted to see. I would have to go back to Lynwood a failure. There would be a note in the *Weekly Index* that "Miss Priscilla Blake, who last month was appointed teacher at Oak Grove School, has just returned home." Then all the dear good women who had sewed tucks and ruffles for my new clothes would rush over to find out why. Susybelle would come gloating and commiserating with Mama. "But they had to have a man teacher," Mama would explain unhappily. "The boys were too much for a girl to manage."

"And all those clothes"—the women would shake their heads sadly—"I was afraid of it."

Before I reached the back gate, Rick had caught up with me. "Whither away so fast? There's a play party tonight at Rance Adler's. Rance sent word to bring everybody and the dog. That includes you."

"Go ahead; take all the dogs," I said coldly. "I don't want to go."

"Not want to go to a play party?" Rick asked, tut-tutting me. "You can't be serious. Page and Hetty are going, but of course, if you insist on staying home, I will stay here with you. I come aco'tin' you, Miss Prissy. I come a fur piece, and I don't aim to leave fo' a spell," he said in a drawling voice.

"I didn't ask you to come."

Rick stood with his back to the gate. "Priscilla Blake, I would like to give you a good shaking," he said angrily. "You don't have to be that hardhearted. I have ridden farther than I ever did to see any girl. Can't you hear my po' heart poundin' fo' you? Can't you see the love light in my eyes?"

"Quit your play-acting and let me through the gate."

He did not budge. "A toll, please. One kiss, and I will

let you go get prettied up. I will admit you do look pretty
awful."

Hetty called from the back porch. "You had better hurry
and get dressed, Prissy. We're all going to the play party,
and we have to go by for the Brocks. Let your feller talk to
Page awhile."

Rick groaned and opened the gate. "But remember, Sister Sue," he said, hissing, "the villain still pursues."

I picked out my fanciest dress and tried to do my hair as
Dozie had done it the day of the parade. It did not look the
same but was not too bad. I rubbed powder on my face to
take away the slick, sunburned look and preened before the
mirror. Dresses and face powder and a fancy hairdo did
change a person's looks. I decided I need not look so awful
all the time.

Rick jumped to his feet and rubbed his eyes when he
saw me. "No, it can't be," he said, "but it is—our Good
Queen Bess. . . . " He made a sweeping bow. "Thy banquet
awaits thee, most noble queen."

Page winked at me. "Your young man is cracked in the
head, Priss. He'll do with watching."

"Not the head, Page," Rick said, moaning, "the heart,
man, the heart!"

Hetty had outdone herself on supper. That Rick was the
son of a probable governor impressed her mightily. That he
had come calling on me impressed her even more. There
were platters of ham and fried chicken. There were beans
and squash and black-eyed peas, egg custard and pumpkin
pie, and two kinds of cake, besides pickles and jelly and
hot biscuits.

Rick groaned when he saw the spread. "It is just too bad
Page Carter saw you first, Hetty, else he'd never have had
a chance." Rick had his father's gift for flattery.

"Why is it, Priscilla," he asked, passing the chicken, "that
I always see you over a loaded table? Do people feel sorry

for you because you are so thin? I'll weigh a ton by the
time I am here a month."

"So you are staying a month, are you? How nice. I won't
be here. I am not teaching at Oak Grove any more."

Page frowned. "What happened, Priss? Did you meet the
preacher after you left me?"

"I met every man this side of Blue Springs who is old
enough to vote. They were having a friendly little poison
powwow in the schoolhouse, just tearing me to shreads when
I burst in on them—in pants, of course, like the hoyden I
am."

"Now that's your dramatic sense, Priss," Richard said,
applauding me. "Nothing like a well-timed entrance. You
are a born actress."

"I am glad I am born for something. I am certainly no
schoolteacher." Mimicking Hack Mifford, I said, "That there
woman ain't fitten to teach my children. No siree, no female
woman that wears pants is going to mislead Hack Mifford's
babes in the woods. And those 'obskeen' charts of the human
body are jest too much for Sandy Goff. Just looking at them
gives him a bad case of cold shudders. Things like that hang
in saloons."

Rick whooped. "Immodest, obscene, and not fitten to
teach young uns. Priscilla Blake, you are a gal after my own
heart. Remind me to marry you tomorrow."

Page and Hetty laughed, but I could see they were disturbed. "What did the preacher say?" Page wanted to know.
"Was he willing for you to go?"

"I don't know about that, but he shut them up in short
order. Dora's pappy must have had something to do with it.
He sat there the whole time laughing to himself, but he
didn't say a word."

Page looked relieved. "Well, don't give up yet. If the
preacher took up for you against that gang, you can expect
something."

"But I have given up. I told them I was through. I am

tired of fighting, Page. I came here to teach, not to fight."

Page laid down his knife and fork. His eyes had an intense look. "You may not have known it, Priss, but you did come here to fight. Fighting is a teacher's job, expecially in back-country schools. You came to fight ignorance because ignorance breeds poverty and greed, and they are the seeds of crime."

"Amen, brother," Rick said fervently. "My sentiments exactly."

Page looked down at his plate for a moment in deep thought. "You may think a teacher in an isolated poor country school doesn't amount to much, that whatever you do makes no difference. But it does. It's people like you who can help: the little country schoolteacher who can teach them that pictures of the liver and intestinal tract are not obscene. It's not so much teaching them to read right as to think right, and you've made a good start." Page rubbed his eyes and sighed. "It may be too late for the Hack Miffords and the Buck Hatters, but you are teaching their children to be different. They'll be running things here in a few years, and they and the country will be better for your teaching." Page looked around surprised. "Why, I never meant to spout off like that," he said.

"I didn't know you were such a speechmaker," Rick said approvingly. "Why don't you run for governor? You'd beat my pappy in a slow walk. I'd even vote for you myself."

Page grinned. "Well, there's one thing that gets me riled up—and that's plain, unadulterated show-off ignorance. You can comb the two territories from one end to the other and not find any more concentrated ignorance anywhere than right here in Oak Grove."

Page pushed back his chair. "The preacher will be here tomorrow. You can depend on that. By the way, Rick brought the mail from Blue Springs, Priss. There's a letter for you. We'll go hitch up the team now."

Chapter 14

R ance and Ora Adler had come from the Canadian River valley. They had married at the big meeting in August and had recently moved to the old Ridley place on Possum Creek. Rance had been wanting a party so they could get acquainted with their neighbors. Rick told us of Rance's invitation. "He's aimin' to put the big pot in the little one," he said, quoting Rance, "and he said he'd feed the crowd if he had to butcher his milk cow. He has a yearling roasting and he sent to town for enough wasp-nest bread to choke a congressman. If the wash kettle breaks down, he promised, he'll boil coffee in the syrup buckets for the crowd, and the dogs can have the bones."

Long before we came near the house, we heard fiddle music and the stomping of feet. The open space in front was filled with wagons, and the dogs were timidly getting acquainted. From the looks of things, everyone had taken

Rance at his word and turned out to dance, eat, and swap talk with their neighbors.

"Well, here we are," Ed Brock said. He climbed over the wheel and helped Hetty down. "Looks like the whole blamed shootin' match is here."

Ed and Page unhooked the team and tied the horses to a tree. Dora skipped about happily in her stiff new shoes and the coat her mother had made from her wedding dress.

"Will you look at that young un?" Effie said proudly. "Her shoes will be all wore out before the new's off of them. But I guess she's been long enough without them."

Hetty gave Dora a spank as she skipped past. "Let her have her fun."

Effie took off her shabby wrap. She looked like a dressed-up little girl in her full-skirted blue-gingham dress and with a red ribbon around her dark hair. The moonlight softened her thin features, and she looked not much older than Dora.

"Is that the dress you stood up in to marry?" I asked.

Effie smoothed her tiny waist. "No'm, this were the first dress Ed ever bought me after we married. He paid for it out of our first picking. He said he were bound to buy me a dress if we had to go hungry. And we might near did, too," she added with a catch in her throat. "But Ed managed."

"Are you going to cut that one up for Dora?" I asked.

"This un? Sakes no, I couldn't do that. Ed were right proud to buy the goods—he picked it hisself. I reckon he likes to see me purtied up."

Rick slipped his hands under her elbows and lifted her quickly until her face was on a level with his. "Ed's right. If you were my woman, I'd keep you prettied up all the time."

Embarrassed, Effie pulled herself away. "Ed don't do too bad," she said stiffly. "We make out right fair. Ed's a proud man of his family and a good worker. I got no cause to complain."

"Rick Harper," I said, scolding him, "quit teasing Effie. Don't pay any attention to him, Effie. He sweet-talks every woman he sees and doesn't mean a word of it."

Ed and Page came up, and we started toward the house. "Miss Prissy," Ed said, "I'm shore proud of the way you lit into that outfit at the schoolhouse. It takes an iron crowbar to make a dent on them feller's heads. But old Preacher Higgins fixed them proper. When Crim Higgins lights in on them, they shet up. I was right pleased you blessed them out. It done a lot of good."

"It's too late to do any good. That was my farewell speech," I said airily.

"No'm, I reckon not. Not yet," Ed drawled. "We don't aim to let the first teacher ever handled that gang get away. We'll keep you if we have to hog-tie you." He caught Dora's hand and pulled her up close. "Dory here'd skin me alive if we let you quit, and I ain't quite ready for that."

Ed looked no older than a boy. He had probably been eighteen or so when he married Effie. He was so thin he looked as if he had not had a full meal in a month, but he had scrubbed and shaved and combed until his face and hair shone in the moonlight. He wore his clean work-clothes easily.

"Ed, tell me something," I said. "The preacher didn't change his tune without good reason. What did you do to him?"

Ed shook with silent laughter. "Who, me? Why, I didn't do a thing to him—not nary a thing."

"All right then, what has the preacher done, Ed," Rick asked, "that he knows you know?"

Ed scanned the night sky. "See that ring around the moon," he said, chuckling. "Jest wouldn't be a bit surprised if it rains by tomorrow night."

Effie giggled, "Aw, Ed, you're a sight!"

If the dance had been an Indian stomp-dance it would have been no noisier. Rance and Ora met us at the door. Redheaded Rance shook hands all around and greeted us exuberantly. "Howdy, folks, howdy. I'm shore glad to see you," he shouted. "I got my neighbors spotted now. I know where to borry seed corn and breakin' plows or a jug of sorghum 'lasses. Come right in, folks, make yourselves at home. Dance or set, whichever pleases you."

He pumped my hand up and down. "So, this here's the new teacher. Gorry Moses, I am shore pleased to meet you, Miss Prissy. I been hearin' about you."

Ora was a plump, pretty girl squeezed tightly into a light summer dress—probably her wedding dress. Her short light-brown hair curled in ringlets over her head.

"What pretty hair you have, Ora. That's the way I'd like mine," I said.

Ora shook her head. "I'm right ashamed of it, but I just got over typhoid last summer and had to have it cut," she explained apologetically.

The house had two rooms and a shed-room kitchen. The few pieces of furniture had been moved out of the front room into the yard to make room for the dancing. Along the sides and at the end of the room planks had been laid across chairs to make benches for those who did not dance. In one corner a man sawed away at a fiddle and called the figures. His poker-faced partner picked a banjo and sang occasionally, his fat stomach jiggling in time with his playing.

"Who's the black-eyed gal staring daggers at you?" Rick asked, nodding toward the back of the room.

Dora giggled. "That's Minnie Roberts. Miss Prissy stole her feller."

"Dora, I did not! He only walked home with us from school yesterday."

Richard scowled. "I'll take care of him if he comes courting you, but if looks will kill, it's an early demise for you, Priss."

"He just happened to be walking our way," I explained. "He was too bashful to say a word."

"That weren't the way of it." Dora persisted impishly. "He sung her a ballad about 'I loved my love but she went away,' and then he waited and walked her home."

"Ha, the singing kind," Rick said sadly, "and I can't sing a note. Show him to me."

I saw Rick was really teasing. "He's not here yet. When he comes, I'll introduce you."

The music stopped, and the caller shouted: "Get your partners, one and all. All join hands and heed my call." Rick grabbed my hand and pulled me into line.

"But I've never danced," I said, protesting. "Take someone else; I'll watch."

But Rick held my hand tightly. My other hand was caught by someone else and we started moving around in a circle. "Don't worry; you'll catch on," Rick shouted. "We'll all go down to Rowser, yippee—ee—ah!"

We bounded around the room. I was swung right and swung left first by one and then by another until I was dizzy. I was dragged in a grand right and a grand left, then ladies forward and ladies back. Then we sashayed. Everyone seemed to know the dance except me, but no one noticed or cared. When the music stopped, Rick caught me; if he hadn't, I would have fallen.

Rick was mopping his brow with one hand and steadying me with the other when someone tapped me on the arm. It was Jim Iders. His pale face was flushed, his eyes slightly red around the rims.

"I been waitin' for you, Miss Prissy. I'm aimin' to dance the next square with you," he announced flatly.

And I had thought the singing boy was bashful. Not

this time. There was even a trace of truculence in his manner. I turned to Rick. "Mr. Harper, I would like you to meet Mr. Iders. He sings." I flashed a teasing grin at Rick. "He sings sad ballads."

"I'm pleased to meet you, Mr. Iders," Rick said easily. "Now run along. I am dancing this dance with Miss Prissy."

Jim Iders turned and deliberately spat his tobacco chew out the door, then wiped his mouth on his sleeve. "I ain't aimin' to have no fight if I can help"—his thin voice was sharply belligerent—"but I aim to dance this dance with Miss Prissy."

Rick clenched his fists, but I shook my head. "Go on and dance with Ora, Rick. She doesn't have a partner."

Rick went off grumbling. Jim stood by waiting for the music to start. I caught a whiff of his breath. "Why, Jim Iders, you've been drinking!"

"Yes, ma'am," Jim said mildly, "I had a few."

I was shocked. "You had a few drinks?"

"A few dipperfuls," Jim corrected me. "Hack Mifford's got a kag out back. He jest teemed it off yesterday, but it's right fair."

"I can't dance with you, Jim, when you're drinking. Go dance with your own girl."

"You're my girl, and I aim to dance with you." He caught my arm and held it tightly.

I looked around for Rick, but he was not in sight. Just then the musicians struck up a lively tune. Jim pulled me into the circle. The caller chanted in time to the music:

> The bird hop out and the crow hop in,
> All join paddies and go 'round again.
> The crow hop out and circle four,
> Do-si-do and do-si-do.

This time I began to see the pattern of the dance and followed through more easily. The men galloped around the room like young colts, helped on, I was sure, by generous dipperfuls from the "kag." The house shook from the impact of heavy boots and shoes.

The music stopped, and the dancers reshuffled. Rick came up to Jim and me. "Now go away," he said to Jim. "Git, and go fast. You have had your dance."

The crack of Jim Iders' knuckles against Rick's chin was sudden. Rick staggered and almost went down, but someone caught him from behind. Jim Iders said mildly, "I told you I wasn't aimin' to have no fight if I could help."

Page caught Rick by one arm and someone else had the other. "We don't want any fights here," Page said admonishingly. "What we do want is some of that good barbecued yearling. Reckon it's about ready, Rance?"

While the men were quieting Rick and Jim, I slipped over and squeezed in beside Hetty. Just then Dora rushed in from outside, bursting with something to tell. She was giggling so much that I could not understand her when she leaned over and whispered something in my ear.

Effie reproached her mildly, but Dora giggled again. "Her feller wants her to step outside."

Hetty shook her head emphatically. "Don't do it, Prissy."

"But her feller's waitin' at the well," Dora said insistantly. "He said it was important to come quick."

"I don't care if he falls in," I told her solemnly, "and he probably will if he waits until I get there."

The small boy who had been staring at me, all eyes, jerked Dora's apron. "Ask her yourself," Dora said. "I told you you'd have to." The child's big eyes clouded. A little redheaded girl who was holding his hand picked up the bottom of her skirt and wiped his nose. "Don't cry, Buddy," she said, "Sissy will ask her."

"What is it?" I was curious to know what the child wanted.

"He wants to see your innards," Sissy whispered shyly.

"What?" I gasped. "Did you say my innards?"

"Yes, ma'am," Sissy whispered. "Them pitchers you got at school. Pap said they was shore purty. Said you could see ever'thing you got inside. Buddy calls them teacher's innards."

I struggled for a straight face. "Come to school Monday. I'll show them to you."

Buddy looked up at his sister questioningly. She put her arm around him. "We'll get up 'fore day, Buddy, and we can foot it by dinner." Buddy was led away, his big eyes grateful and happy.

Effie came back from dancing with Ed. She was flushed and laughing, but Ed looked pale and tired. I stood up. "Take my place, Ed; I'll probably dance the next dance."

"No, ma'am, thanky, but I'll jest squat a minute." And he squatted, leaning against Effie's knees, breathing heavily.

"Why, Ed, you've plumb wore yourself out." Effie scolded him, smoothing his sandy hair affectionately. "You shouldn't a done it. I plumb forgot your slow breath."

"I wish they'd play something pretty now, like 'Picking Cherries,'" Hetty said. "I used to dance that when I was a girl."

Ed unfolded his long legs and stood up. "I reckon the fiddler knows that tune. If he don't, I'll whistle it till he catches on. You'd better dance that one with your feller, Miss Prissy. It's real nice."

Ed and the fiddler went to work busily on the new tune, Ed whistling and the fiddler experimentally trying it out until he caught on and fiddled away confidently.

Suddenly Jim Iders bolted through the open door, wild-eyed and red of face. Rick, his hair disheveled and a bluish bruise on his chin, was hard on his heels.

"Oh, Miss Prissy," Jim blurted out. "I'm aimin' to dance the Cherry Dance with you."

"You'll do nothing of the kind," Rick said, growling. "If

you've not had enough, step outside again. I will dance the Cherry Dance with Miss Prissy."

"No, Miss Prissy," Jim said, panting, "I aim to——"

But before he could finish, Minnie Roberts, Jim's black-eyed girl, bore down on us like a charging bull, her face red and her eyes shooting sparks. She pushed herself in front of Jim. "You quit trying to take my feller," she screamed. "Ain't no citified schoolma'am going to take my man jest when he's got marryin' in his head. You leave him alone, Miss Priss-Ike." With that she caught him by the arm and marched him away. He struggled ineptly against her determination.

When I could stop laughing, I said weakly, "Mr. Harper, will you please, sir, kindly, sir, dance the Cherry Dance with me, whatever it is?"

Page came to claim Hetty for the dance. "It's a real pretty dance, Priss, but it has a surprise ending," he said in warning.

The Cherry Dance was pretty. The movements were grace-ful as a Virginia reel. The dancers moved lightly, with more dignity than before and no rowdy galloping around. The surprise came at the end when each man suddenly lifted his partner high in the air. Rick swung me up and held me for a second at arm's length. Then, before I knew what was coming, he lowered me and kissed me full on the lips.

I was furious, but Rick laughed heartily. "That's part of the dance, Priss; the best part. That's picking the cherries. A fellow dances it with his best girl so he can steal a kiss."

"You didn't have to do it."

Rick grinned. "Of course I didn't have to do it. I wanted to. Would you rather it had been Jim Iders?"

With that I grinned back. "I'd rather have a plate of bar-becue right now," I answered.

Chapter 15

*R*ick *had to leave for Blue Springs soon after breakfast.*
"Dad will be pacing the floor," he said, "but I want to see
your schoolhouse before I go."

"I'll ride that far with you and show you the shortcut
through the woods to the main road," I offered.

Rick shook his head doubtfully. "I'd like you to, but after what I saw last night at that Rowser party, I am not
so sure it is safe for you to come back alone, Priss."

"But Dora and I walk it every day, Rick."

"It will be all right," Page said, "but you had better get
back as soon as you can, Priss. I look for the preacher
almost any time."

Rick had rolled his good clothes in his slicker and tied
the roll behind his saddle. Even the new derby was neatly
stowed away. In his flannel shirt and unpressed pants he
looked more at home in the saddle.

We pulled the horses down to a walk when we came to

the rutted woods road. The crunch of their hooves on the dead leaves was the only sound in the crisp morning air.

"Priss," Rick said suddenly, a worried look in his eyes, "I am serious. I won't have an easy minute until you leave this place. With some of the men what they are around here, anything could happen. I don't like it."

I laughed. "Why, Rick, what could happen here? There's nobody but a handful of poor farmers and their families. It is all they can do to make enough to keep alive. I feel sorry for them; they are so ignorant and helpless."

"They are not so helpless, even if they are ignorant, Priss. Remember what Page said about ignorance breeding crime?"

"I am not worrying about that, Rick, but I do worry about the children. If the new state does not build some decent schools in the backwoods, they will grow up to be just as ignorant as their parents. But don't worry about me. Nothing is going to happen to me if I stay, and I probably won't."

"Use your head, Priss," Rick said. "There's plenty that could happen here. You weren't born yesterday." He pulled the spirited paint down to a slow walk, curbing him with a single movement of his knee. "These men, Priss—the Sandy Goffs and the Hack Miffords—they hate you. Do you know why? Because you make them realize how sorry they are, how shiftless and inferior they are before a real woman, and they don't like it. To them you are not the tomboy you think yourself. You are a very pretty woman."

"But they are married. They have families to think about."

"Sure, they are married, and their wives are worn-out drudges. The wives will hate you, too, because you make them seem so drab and homely. Take Jim Iders' girl. She hates you because Jim likes you better."

"Don't make me afraid, Rick," I said protestingly. "I might even be afraid of you."

Rick reached over and turned my face toward him. "For Pete's sake, Priss, be sensible. You are safe enough with me, but that is because I am falling in love with you. I didn't know until last night. That fool Jim Iders made me see it."

I stared at him in disbelief. His eyes no longer had the teasing, impudent look so characteristic of them. They were almost sad.

"I guess I had better get along," I said abruptly.

Rick caught Daisy's bridle. "Priss, I am generally a fool, and I know it, but I am dead serious now." He laid his hand over mine on the pommel of the saddle. "Prissy, I am not asking how you feel about me, but there'll come a time when I will." He squared his shoulders. Suddenly his eyes twinkled with fun again. "Dad's going to kill me sure for keeping him waiting, Priss. We'd better get going."

At the door of the schoolhouse Rick looked around in distaste. "This is a disgrace, Priss. It's much worse than I thought. How do you stand it?"

"Sir, I'll have you know you are talking about my schoolhouse," I said with mock severity, then I laughed. "It's clean, Rick; Dora and I sweep it every day."

Rick caught my hand. "Priss, go home. Don't come back another day. We would not let our horses stay in a place like this."

"But I am a schoolteacher, not a horse. There is a difference. This is what they expect the teacher to teach in." I walked back toward the horses.

Rick closed the door with a bang and followed me. "I really have to be going, Priss. We have a long way to go today." He put his foot in the stirrup and then turned back. "It's funny, Priss, I don't like to say good-bye. Yesterday I would not have cared."

When I turned to wave where the road forked, Rick was still watching, his fine dark eyebrows drawn together in a deep frown.

I road back along the quiet woods road, drowsing in the early morning sunlight, letting Daisy choose her own gait. Rick had been so serious. "Nothing can happen to me here; that's silly," I had said, but suddenly the woods did not seem so friendly. I looked around apprehensively and tightened Daisy's slack reins just in time. A shabby tramp of a man, a rusty black-felt hat pulled over his eyes, had sprung from the bushes and tried to catch the bridle. Good old Daisy jumped sidewise out of reach of his clutching hand, and had I not been a split second ahead of her, I would have landed in the road. With a sharp kick from me Daisy bolted. When I slowed her down and looked back, the man had disappeared. The man was Buck Hatters.

Page was waiting at the back gate when I rode up. "The preacher has come and gone. He seemed relieved not to find you here," Page added, "but you are to stay on another month and see how things work out, and you are not to pay any mind to what was said at the meeting yesterday."

"But I can't very well stay, Page. I told them I was quitting. I don't like the things they said about me."

"That's what I told the preacher. I said he couldn't expect you to stay after what those yapping coyotes said, but he said he'd take care of them and see that they left you alone."

I looked over the fields towards the woods. A chill wind was rising, and the sky was fast becoming overcast. There would probably be rain before night, as Ed Brock had predicted. When it rained, the trip to school was a soggy ordeal and the drafty log building cold and damp. The preacher might keep Hack Mifford and the others from talking at the meeting, but he could not control their comings and goings. They could still sneak in and out of the schoolhouse whenever they chose, for crops were in and there was nothing to keep them busy.

Page was watching me, his face set in grim lines. Over

in the pasture his horse nickered. Daisy answered, her head high and her small satiny ears thrust forward.

"Rick says it's not safe for me here, Page. He's afraid something might happen."

"What could happen here, Priss, could happen in Lynwood or any other place. You're no coward, and you're nobody's fool."

Suddenly Daisy jumped, rearing stiffly on her hind legs. I had to catch the saddle horn and hang on until I could get my balance and she had quieted down. Old Wolf had decided to join us.

"Priss, watch for that trick of Daisy's. She's a good mare, but she'll shy at her own shadow. I'd hate for her to throw you. She hates that dog, so keep an eye on her when he's around."

I laughed and felt better. "Papa said you had to know the tricks of horses and men before you could manage them. I know that trick, Page. You warned me the first time I rode Daisy." I slipped down and handed him the reins. "I'm staying. If I can learn Daisy's trick, I can learn those of the men around here."

Chapter 16

A week of changeable November weather passed, and by the next Sunday the norther that had struck on Friday had blown itself out. The sky was clear as a bell, and it was cold enough to redden noses and keep a person on the move outdoors. The dogs had piled up on the sunny side of the chimney, basking in the warmth.

"It's cold enough for hog-killing," Page announced at breakfast. "I'll get Ed over tomorrow, and we'll kill a couple. We could use some fresh meat."

"It's also cold enough for a wolf hunt," I reminded him. "Remember, you promised."

"Yes, it sure enough is, and if I can get that stubborn colt so I can ride him today, we'll have one. The bay has picked up a limp, and I won't be riding him for a spell."

I followed him outside, saying, "Get on with the colt-breaking, then. I am ready for the hunt."

"The new doctor just might come over," Page said. "I

told him we'd run wolves the first cold day, and he wants in on it."

I resented the doctor's wanting to horn in on our wolf hunt. A greenhorn would spoil it. "Dudes have no business running wolves," I announced. "He'd probably fall off the horse."

"You're determined not to like the doctor, aren't you, Priss? What's the matter? He's a real nice fellow."

"Sounds too nice to me," I said. "He must be a sissy."

Page guffawed. "You'll change your tune when you know him. Doc's anything but a sissy."

I climbed the rail fence to watch Page saddle the colt. It was a beautiful black two-year-old with a white star on its forehead. Page had taken it in on a debt. It was bad-tempered and needed riding, he said. "He's full of meanness, and I have to get it out of him before he's any good. He's broken to ride, but he has everybody bluffed." The colt danced around Page, trying to keep away from the saddle blanket.

"If you are going to try to ride him, I'd better get Ed to help," I said.

"Try to ride him?" Page said, snorting. "Try to ride him! I am going to ride him, Priss. Didn't you know Indians are born on horses?"

"Don't Indians ever get thrown?" I jeered.

Hetty had taken an old flannel shirt of Page's and cut it down for me, and she had seamed up a pair of his old woolen pants. Over this amazing outfit I wore the faded jeans jumper that had belonged to Page. With my hair stuffed into an ancient black-felt hat, so that not much but my nose showed, I would have made a good scarecrow. Page had whooped when he saw me. "Say, kid, you make a better boy than a lady any day."

The colt kept Page on the move. I wanted to get in and help, but Page would not let me. "The colt is a fine piece of horseflesh, and would be a runner, but he's a bad actor. When he learns to behave, maybe I'll let you ride him."

"No thanks; I'll keep Daisy." I hooked my feet under the top rail. Page cinched the saddle girth tight and with one swift movement was in the saddle. The colt went wild and bucked all over the lot. I shouted myself hoarse, afraid that at every jump Page would come off. Suddenly I felt a sharp slap on my shoulder.

"Hey, Sonny, ready for a wolf hunt?" a deep voice asked.

I almost went over backwards. It was the new doctor. Just as I had thought, he had come to the wolf chase in a fancy suit, a checked vest, and a black derby. Only a dude doctor would do that. I tried to answer, but the only sound I made was a grunt.

The doctor's dark eyes crinkled with laughter. "Where's your father?"

"Who?" I croaked.

"Page Carter. Isn't he your father?"

I pointed to Page just as the colt came swooping out from behind the corncrib, stifflegged and bucking every step, but with Page still on top.

"Oh, there he is." The doctor opened the gate, and jerking his thumb toward Page, said, "Bet you couldn't do that, Sonny."

"Huh!" I yelled. "I'll bet you——" but I did not finish, for it suddenly occurred to me that the last thing I wanted was for the doctor to know that the scarecrow on the fence was Priscilla Blake. I wanted to get away from there quickly, before he knew I was not Page Carter's boy and could ride a bucking bronco. My throat got tight, and my stomach tied up in knots in a queer feeling that translated itself into a strange yearning for curls and lace ruffles, for a peaches-and-cream complexion and slim lily-white hands. I stared at my grubby paws, chapped and grimy and red with cold, nails stubby and broken, then crammed them into my pockets. I looked at my feet, and my face burned. I wore ladies' buttoned shoes. I hoped he had not seen them.

But something was happening to Page. The colt made a wild leap, reared up on his hind legs, and threw himself sidewise. The doctor ran toward him.

"Hey," I squawked, "watch out, or you'll get killed."

But the colt crawfished, then went for the moon and came down stifflegged. Page sailed over the horse's head and landed in a heap. I held my breath. Page did not move. The doctor fanned at the colt with his derby to scare him away, for he was bucking all over the lot, trying to get rid of the saddle.

"Keep that horse away," he shouted as he knelt beside Page.

"Is Page hurt?" I was almost afraid to ask.

"I don't know, but get that horse out of here, and go for help. We have to get him to the house."

I caught the colt's reins as he bucked past the shed and wrapped them around a post, pulling him up tight. I held him there while I loosened the girth and pulled the saddle off. Relieved of the saddle, the colt quieted down, and I turned him into the calf lot. Then I went over the rail fence.

"Tell Mrs. Carter to heat some water," the doctor called, "and get back here in a hurry, both of you, unless there's someone else to help."

I ran. Page might be hurt pretty bad, for he had not moved. He might even be. . . . Quick tears blinded me, and I ducked my head and ran faster—and plunged headlong into Preacher Higgins. I could have hugged him, I was so glad to see him. Nothing short of Providence could have sent Preacher Higgins at that particular moment. He had a strange, half-wild reproachful look in his eyes.

"The colt's bucked Page off," I said between gasps. "The doctor's there and needs help to bring him in."

The preacher's thin lips moved, but no words came out. He turned and strode off towards the lot, his long legs going like winding blades and the tails of his coat flapping in the wind.

I took a long wheezing thankful breath, but telling Hetty would not be easy. And the doctor had said to hurry. Hetty was icing a cake for dinner, her ruffled pink-calico apron over a brown alpaca dress. Even in her kitchen apron Hetty looked nice enough for church.

I broke the news in one breath. "The colt threw Page. He's hurt."

Hetty set the bowl of icing on the table and carefully laid the knife on it so it would not drip. She wiped her face with her apron and sat down, her hands shaking.

"What's that, Priss?" she whispered, her eyes scared.

"Page is hurt, but the doctor is with him. He wants hot water."

Hetty picked up the steaming kettle and started for the door.

"No, Hetty." I took the kettle from her. "They'll bring him to the house. The preacher's helping."

Hetty stood by, frightened and pale, while the doctor and Preacher Higgins lay Page on the bed.

"Don't worry, Mrs. Carter," the doctor said cheerfully. "He's just had the wind knocked out of him." He pulled up a chair beside the bed. "But I want to look at this ankle. He twisted it when he fell."

The doctor worked off Page's boot and peeled off his sock. He was poking around the ankle when Page opened his eyes and looked around. He grinned weakly. "And I thought I could ride a horse."

The doctor laughed. "Sure you can, Carter, but I told you that horse had killed a man. He's a bad one, but you'll be back in the saddle in a week and never know the difference." The doctor turned to me. "Trot out and get my pill bags,

Sonny. They are in my buggy out front. But keep away from the horses' heels. They're nervous."

The doctor's rig really dazzled me. I had not seen one like it since Banker Spate had bought one in Lynwood. Hitched to the shiny new red-wheeled, rubber-tired buggy was the finest pair of bays I had ever seen. The doctor must have spent all his spare time brushing them. I took the pill bags to the doctor and went to my room.

Page was right. I was determined not to like the doctor. I told myself he was a sissy and a dude, but I knew it was not true. I wished I could show him I could ride a bucking horse, but I could hear Mama saying, "Priscilla, for my sake, do try to be a lady."

Hetty opened the door, bringing a bucket of hot water. "You'd better get cleaned up, Prissy. I've asked the doctor to stay to dinner. Page is all right, but he has to stay in bed a few days."

I swallowed hard. "Hetty, I was scared to death he was——"

"I know," she said soberly. "So was I. But do get prettied up. It's too bad the doctor and the preacher had to see you like this. Get your pretty dress on. Let them see how nice you can look."

"Does the doctor know I'm not——"

Hetty laughed. "I don't believe so, but hurry up. I won't tell him."

Of all the new clothes that Mama had made, nothing was just right. I fussed around and looked at everything I had. I hated my hair because it would not make curls on my forehead. I remembered Susybelle's pretty milk-white skin and pink cheeks and envied her like sin. My face was still dark from summer sunburn. I decided I would wear the green-broadcloth skirt and the pink-frilled blouse that I had declared to high heaven I would never be caught in.

I waited for Hetty to call me, trying to rub my hands

soft with rose water and glycerine. When Hetty introduced
the doctor to me, I tried to remember the way Mama acted
that made men fall over each other to do things for her.
But instead of being a sweet clinging vine, I knew I was
nothing but a gawky tomboy who could twist a grown boy
to his knees. It was no use. I was even tongue-tied like a
schoolboy.

The doctor bowed politely. "Well, this is a surprise. I
thought the young lady teacher had gone home, or I would
certainly have been here before now."

I managed to say something which I hoped nobody had
heard. Hetty chattered away like a magpie, trying to help
me out. Before Hetty could take her place, Preacher Higgins
stalked in, glared at me, and took the chair beside me
where Hetty had meant the doctor to sit.

The meal was a miserable one for me. The doctor and
Hetty carried on the conversation, but I could think of nothing to say, only mumbling, "Yes, thank you," and "No,
thank you," when things were passed to me. When we finished dinner, I went straight to my room, furious at myself. Why did I have to act such a simpleton? What did I
care what the doctor thought of me? I would be going home
soon and would not see him anymore. But I knew that I
did care and I did not want to go home. For the first time
I wanted a man to like me because I was a woman. I
wanted to be beautiful, and I wanted the doctor to know I
was.

Chapter 17

I missed the excitement of Thanksgiving at home. It was a quiet day, with no one to eat Hetty's bountiful dinner but Page, Hetty, and me. Ed Brock took his family to Blue Springs for the day. Hetty had invited the doctor when he had come by Tuesday to check on Page's ankle, but he doubted he could make it, what with the epidemic of grippe and babies. He promised to try.

Dr. Ashton did arrive around four o'clock. I had spent most of the morning trying to do something about my hair and nails without much success. Hetty told me to wear the green plaid. "The doctor will like it," she said. "It goes well with your hair."

When the doctor came, Hetty immediately took him to the dining room.

"Just some coffee and a piece of pie," he said, but when Hetty took the white cover from the table and he saw a complete Thanksgiving dinner, he sighed happily. "How did you know, Mrs. Carter, that I really cannot remember when I last ate?"

"I knew you'd had no food. A country doctor never has time for a decent meal, especially when he doesn't have a wife to look out for him."

"You're right. Why, I haven't even had time to look at a pretty girl lately, until now." He smiled at me. "Please sit down and talk to me, Miss Prissy."

When Hetty came in, bringing steaming coffee and pumpkin pie, he said, his eyes twinkling, "By the way, I haven't seen that young boy around here. Where is he, and where is Page?"

"Page is over in the pasture, I guess," Hetty replied, and then added innocently, "and I haven't seen the boy lately, either, have you, Priss?"

I could have bumped her. "No, I haven't," I said emphatically.

"That's too bad. I liked that young fellow," the doctor said, pushing back his chair. "Mrs. Carter, you have been a lifesaver. I am sorry to leave now, but I have more calls to make. If Miss Prissy will come along, I would like to walk to the end of the lane and back." He looked at Hetty slyly. "I need the exercise, you know."

"Exercise it is, ha!" Hetty said, laughing.

Once out of the house he took my hand. "May I drop the 'Miss,' Prissy? You know you are like a breath of spring to a weary country doctor." We walked along silently for a while, then he said, "I hear your young man has been here—what's his name? Harper?"

"Richard Harper. Only he's not my young man; he's just a friend."

The doctor turned toward me. His eyes had little tired lines around them. I had not known they were so gray, so steady, so disconcerting. I had never really looked at them before.

"Prissy," he said softly, "there is so much I want to say to you. Someday soon I hope I may, but now is not the time nor the place. You're a dear child—almost a woman." He sighed, and we turned back toward the house. "Ah, well, when a doctor has to choose between duty and pleasure, he must always choose duty." We were back at the hitching post. He took both my hands and kissed me, then untied the bays and drove away.

Hetty was waiting for me at the door.

"Did you see him kiss me, Hetty—that nice fatherly kiss?" I asked in exasperation.

"It didn't surprise me," she said. "But there's a letter from Rick that Ed Brock brought while the doctor was eating."

I walked over to the mirror and looked at my reflection. I did not like what I saw. My hair, which I had so carefully twisted and coiled on top of my head to make me look older, was hanging straight and disheveled about my shoulders. "You're a dear child," I said, mimicking the doctor.

"Read your letter," Hetty urged. "Maybe it will cool you off."

"But I told Rick not to write me," I said, protesting. Now I was glad he had. At least he would not think me a child. I opened the letter and began reading.

Dear Prissy,

I know you told me not to write, but I must. I can't read, study nor sleep for thinking of you. Priss, I can't wait any longer to ask you. I want you to marry me. Please, Priss, I love you very much and have never wanted anything in my life so much as to have you say you will marry me.

I can't be with you Thanksgiving, but I will be in Lynwood for the Christmas holidays and

I will be with you every day and minute you will let me. I hope you can give me my answer then. The wedding would have to be next summer. By then I will be twenty-one and will get an inheritance from my Grandfather that will see us through my last year at the university. Oh, Prissy, I do love you so—please say yes.

Rick

P.S. I have spoken to your father about my intentions.

Tears streamed down my face. I handed the letter to Hetty.

Hetty read it and put her arms around me. "Which will it be, Prissy?" she asked, wiping her eyes, "The doctor or Rick?"

I fumbled for a handkerchief. "I don't know. I just don't know. 'Such a dear child,' " I stormed. Then my tears began again.

Chapter 18

The rain that settled into a steady downpour Saturday afternoon stopped Sunday night. After two days of bright sunshine the calendar got itself mixed up, and it was spring again. The days were so warm the children came barefooted to school, and it was hard to believe it was December. Things were too calm and quiet for peace of mind. I had become so accustomed to interference that its absence worried me. But I should have known that, like the false spring, the calm and quiet of Oak Grove could not last.

After the noon recess on Thursday Izzy Mifford was proudly reading about Ned and his dog to the first reader class. Suddenly, over Izzy's hesitant but determined recitation, came the sound of music from directly overhead, where the rusty stovepipe was threaded through a flimsy tin flue in the roof. Mournful and sweet came the melancholy quavers of "I loved my love and she went away," plus all

the trimmings and trills possible on a harmonica played
by a master.

Annoyed at the interruption, I laid down my book and
went outside. The children followed. Straddling the ridgepole of the schoolhouse roof was Jim Iders. His skinny
elbows worked up and down in time to the music, and his
thin jeans-clad legs, bowed out to keep his balance, gave
him the look of a giant grasshopper ready to jump.

"Jim Iders, come down off that roof," I called. "You are
disturbing my school. What a silly thing for you to do."

But Jim neither saw nor heard me. Without losing a
breath he went from the sad notes of "I loved my love"
into a rollicking rowdy hoedown tune. The children were
delighted. Instantly the infectious melody went to their
heads and heels, and they galloped around the school yard
like a bunch of young goats. They shouted words in time
to the crazy tune. Jim seemed totally unaware of his audience. He played one tune after another while I stood help-
lessly, begging him to quit and trying to corral the ex-
uberant children. It was no use. After yelling myself
hoarse and getting nowhere, I sat down on the doorsill and
laughed until I was weak.

When both the music and the children were at the
wildest, a buggy drove up. It was Mr. Brending, the Lynwood school principal. Neither Jim nor the children saw
him, and the earsplitting hubbub never wavered a note.

Mr. Brending tied up his horse and looked around at
the frenzied pupils of the Oak Ridge School. That he should
see them and me like this embarrassed and humiliated me.
I had wanted him to be proud of me.

"What's this, Priscilla?" he shouted over the din.

I shook my head sadly.

"A good musician up there," he yelled, "but a hazardous
spot for performing, I think. What's the occasion?"

Before I could answer, a whirlwind struck in our midst.

A disheveled female, yowling like a wildcat, her arms flailing the air, landed between us. It was Jim Iders' black-haired girl, Minnie Roberts.

Minnie sprang at me, screeching, "You can't have my Jim. I'll tear your hair out." And if Mr. Brending had not caught her, she would have made a good try.

"What's this all about?" he asked, struggling with the battling girl, losing his hat and getting clawed in the face for his trouble.

"That Miss Priss-Ike's trying to take my feller," Minnie screamed above the rollicking music. "I'll scratch her eyes out."

"Now, wait a minute," Mr. Brending said, pinning her arms behind her. "You are not going to do anything of the kind. Let's get this straightened out. Do you know what the trouble is, Priscilla?"

The children had gathered around us and were watching and listening with big eyes and open mouths. Up on the roof Jim Iders was working away on his harmonica.

"She's Minnie Roberts. She wants to marry Jim Iders, up on the roof." My face burned. Not enough to be caught in this ridiculous situation, but I had to bobble my rhetoric.

Mr. Brending roared. "Well, we don't mind her marrying him on the roof or anywhere else, just so long as she leaves you alone."

"She thinks I want Jim."

Mr. Brending gave Minnie a little push. "Now, Miss Minnie, get your man down and run along. I have business with Miss Priscilla, and I can't hear myself think."

Minnie called to Jim to come down, but Jim did not hear. He worked away like an old fiddler at a country picnic. Minnie ordered him down, begged, then threatened, but Jim plainly did not want to hear.

"I'll get him," she screamed, and ran towards the woods. In a few minutes she was back, dragging an old makeshift ladder. This she hoisted against the schoolhouse wall. "If I have to come up there for you, Jim Iders, I'll maul you to pieces." She started up the rickety ladder. Jim saw her coming and stood up, tottering toward the end of the roof.

"Don't you dare jump," Minnie yelled. As she lunged for him Jim made a wild leap, hit the ground running, and was off through the woods like a deer. Minnie scrambled back down the ladder and took off after him. We watched the chase until they were out of sight.

Mr. Brending wiped his scratched face. "A woman after my own heart," he said, grinning. "A real old-fashioned clinging vine."

He did not stay long. He explained he had been asked to make a survey of the schools throughout the area, and it was plain to see that Oak Grove School was not fit for use. "It will have to be closed by Christmas or before, depending on the weather. It won't be reopened until another building is put up, probably late spring."

I suppose he noticed my doleful look. "Don't feel too bad about it, Prissy. There are other schools needing teachers."

Dora and I did not have much to say on the way home.

"I wish he hadn't come," she finally blurted out. "I wish he'd stayed away."

"You had better be glad he did. My eyes would have been scratched out if he had not."

Dora sighed. "That Minnie sure is in love with Jim, for a fact." She looked at me impishly. "Looks as if she's going to beat your time, Miss Prissy."

"Well, I hope she marries him in a hurry. I don't want to run into her again soon."

And she did. On Saturday morning a man rode up to the Carter's gate and said Minnie and Jim had married Friday

and wanted us to come to their "enfair" that night. We
didn't go. I began packing my trunk.

I faced the last week of school glumly. I had become attached to the shabby little log house and the shabbier children. I would miss them and the little gray squirrel that
sometimes peered through the chinking and set the children laughing hilariously. I would not soon forget the lanky
old razorback sow rummaging for acorns in the woods
around the school, nor would I forget the zooming, busi-
ness-like yellow jackets we respectfully let alone on the
sills of the little windows.

On Wednesday afternoon just before four Dr. Ashton
stopped by the school to give Dora and me a ride home, as
he had several times before when he had had a call in the
neighborhood. I dismissed the children, and Dora and I
were soon settled in the shining road-buggy under a warm
lap robe.

Hetty was delighted to see the doctor and ushered us into
the little parlor, which was pleasantly warm after the bit-
ing wind. "You two sit and talk," she said, "while I stir
up the fire and get supper. You are going to stay, aren't
you?"

"That was my ulterior motive for bringing Miss Priscilla home," he said with a broad wink at me. He settled
back in a chair. "I had forgotten there could be such comfort." For a few minutes he sat with his head back and
eyes closed. I thought he was asleep and was about to slip
away.

"Don't go," he said, opening his eyes. "I was just enjoy-
ing a chance to relax. Such a luxury."

He began to tell me about his home in Kentucky in a
fair-sized town. He was orphaned at ten, and Dr. Ben
Kirk had adopted him and educated him, sending him to

medical school. He was planning to finish here in the late spring and go back to Kentucky to work with Dr. Ben.

"You would like Kentucky," he said. "It is a land of beautiful women and fine horses—but the beautiful women always come first."

I had a strange feeling of jealousy—almost resentment —for these unknown beautiful women. I wondered if one were waiting for him.

When the doctor left, after having had one of Hetty's bountiful meals, he took my hands and held them for a minute. "I'll be thinking of you, Priss, in the months ahead; will you think occasionally of me?"

On the last day, after the hugs and "Good-bye, teacher" from the children, Dora and I closed the door of the little log schoolhouse. Neither of us could trust ourselves to speak until we were almost at the end of the lane. Then Dora stopped, put both arms around me, and broke into sobs.

"Miss Prissy, don't go. Marry the doctor and stay here, even if we don't have a school."

I was crying, too, but I tried to laugh. "I couldn't if I tried. He doesn't want me."

"Pappy'll find out," she said hopefully. "If he do, will you stay?"

"If he *does*, not *do*, Dora."

"Goody, goody, I'll tell Pappy you said you'd stay if he do." And I could not catch her to tell her I did not mean what she thought.

Chapter 19

It was good to be home again, especially at Christmas.
Mama was in the kitchen when Papa and I got there.

"You look well, Priscilla, but you've changed. What's happened?" she asked. "Are you in love?"

I laughed. "So much has happened, Mama, I couldn't begin to tell you. Am I in love? I—I—don't think so."

"Richard Harper is coming tomorrow," she announced.

"Yes, I know. He wrote." I perched on the kitchen stool and watched her stirring up the coals in the range to heat coffee for Papa.

Pinky came in noisily. I tried to kiss him, but he backed away. "You wanna ride Zade? She's in the pasture," he said breathlessly. "This fella said——"

"No, Pinky, I have other things to do now."

"Gosh, old schoolteacher," he grumbled as he stamped out.

"Dr. Rutherford expects you to announce your engagement—you and Richard." Mama was not easily distracted.

"But we are not engaged."

Mama sat down limply. "Why, Priscilla, Richard asked your father—" She wiped her eyes and stared at me.

"Only for permission to court her, Sally." Papa had come in and was pouring a cup of coffee. "You see, there's this young doctor——"

"Doctor?" Mama echoed. "What young doctor? Why didn't you tell me about him?"

"There is really nothing to tell, Mama. He practices out of Blue Springs."

"How old is he? Is he good-looking? Has he proposed?" Mama asked all at once.

"No, he has not proposed," I said patiently. "He is older than Richard—almost thirty, I think—and yes, I think he is good-looking. His name is Dale Ashton." I took a piece of cake. "I am going to change now."

When I came down, Judge Harper and Richard were in the parlor. "Why, Priscilla, what a young lady you have become—long skirts and hair up." The Judge beamed as he kissed me. "And pretty, too!"

Rick pushed him aside. "Hey, Dad, Prissy is my girl." As he started to kiss me I ducked, and the kiss landed squarely on my nose. "Remember? I am the fellow who wants to marry you."

The Judge laughed. "Very inexpert, son. You will have to do better than that."

At that moment Mama came bustling in with a tray of cookies and a steaming pot of tea. She set the tray down. "Now, Priscilla, will you bring in the cups and sugar and cream? Richard will help you, I am sure."

Richard kissed Mama on the cheek. "Sally Blake, you are a most understanding woman."

He took my arm and marched me into the kitchen. "Very inexpert, ha!" he muttered. "He should see this one."

But Pinky forestalled that one by bursting through the back door, yelling, "Sis, this fella said—" When he saw Richard, he stopped, his mouth open.

Richard took him by the shoulders and propelled him into the hall. "This fella said go get yourself some cookies —in the parlor. Now go!"

He came back, and I handed him cups and saucers. "I'll bring the cream," I said.

"Tantalizing woman," he grumbled. "But I warn you, the villain will still pursue you."

At supper Rick kept everyone laughing with his account of the Rowser party and my singing swain, Jim Iders.

"I am really jealous of that man. But that girl of his, Minnie, is a black-haired tigress. I hope she gets him."

"She did, just before I left."

Rick gave a sigh of relief. "Thank goodness for that."

The Judge left early—business letters to write, he explained.

"Dad, that's really a great idea," Rick said. "I would not think of detaining you. Do let me get your coat and hat."

The Judge came over to tell me goodnight, saying, "Be good to Rick, Prissy; he teases a lot, but he loves you very much."

Mama decided she had better go clean up the dishes and went to the kitchen, followed by Papa and Pinky, leaving Rick and me alone in the firelit parlor.

"Prissy," Rick said, "that love seat there by the fire was just made for us. Now, Prissy, I wouldn't for the world have you think I am impatient, but please, won't you say you will marry me? I have tried to tell you how much I love you."

I watched the glowing embers drop from the burning logs. Rick was such fun to be with—interesting, entertaining, a tease—and there was no doubt I was very fond of him. But marriage needed more than fondness. Did I love him enough? The embers turned to gray ash. Love had to be more than the warm glow that came with a kiss.

"I don't know, Rick; I am just not sure."

Rick held my hand tightly. "Is it that doctor, Priss, at Oak Grove?" His dark eyes were pleading, serious, almost sad.

"Rick, I really don't know. I do know that I am very fond of you and that I admire and respect the doctor very much. But I am not sure I know what love is."

"Priss, love is so many things it would take a lifetime to tell you. That is what I want; a lifetime with you to tell you, to show you, what love is." He stood up, looking at the fire. Suddenly he took the poker and jabbed at the logs until the sparks flew and quick flames shot up. "That's better," he said. "I don't like dying fires.

"All right, Prissy, I said I would not rush you. Any girl has a right to expect to be courted before she commits herself. I have not had much chance, but come tomorrow I'll be here bright and early, prepared to give you such a co'tin' as no gal ever had before. It's getting late. I guess I had better go."

I stood by my bedroom window a long time, looking out at the millions of stars. Rick was watching the same stars as he walked back to the hotel. And was the doctor, I wondered, watching them at Blue Springs or Oak Grove?

Soon after breakfast Rick was at the door, in old shoes and wearing a bright plaid-flannel shirt.

"Get into your old duds," he said. "We're going pecan-hunting. I expect your mother could use some in her baking."

The morning was sunny and crisp. We found a big tree in the middle of a field with nuts scattered over the ground. We soon filled our baskets. Back home Mama was just setting out dinner. Boiled pork ribs and dumplings, baked sweet potatoes and milk.

"Fit for a king," Richard declared. "Now, Priscilla and I will do the dishes."

"No," Mama said. "You and Priscilla shell your pecans. I will be needing some of them."

As we sat on the porch in the sun, shelling the nuts, Rick told me about his work at the university and his plans after he had finished. "And they all include you," he added.

The days went quickly, with long walks, parties, Christmas-tree trimming at the church, visits to Doc's. On Christmas Eve Rick brought me a little package wrapped in tissue paper and tied with gold cord.

"For my girl," he said.

The gift was a tiny gold watch with a bowknot pin of gold and green enamel.

"Rick, it is beautiful. I have never had a watch, and I am not sure I should accept so lovely a present from you."

"Take it, Priss. Wear it always, and when you look at it, remember it's time to say 'yes.'"

Chapter 20

One windy March day I came home to find a letter from Page. The trustees wanted me to finish the school term. The county had built a new schoolhouse, and there were new blackboards and plenty of chalk and erasers. There was a drilled well and a pump, a new stove, and wood enough to last six months, although Page said I would not likely need that much. But what was most important, there was money enough for three months' school. Would I come back and teach?

I could hardly believe it. Papa said it might not be a bad idea, because I was going to have to do something to get that place out of my system. I had done nothing but talk about it since I came home.

The trip back to Oak Grove was not like the first one. This time I could hardly wait to get there. Before I left, I went to Miss Eva's, our best milliner, and bought a hat that surprised even Mama. No doubt she had expected me

143

to come home with a cowboy hat, but this one was of cream-colored straw trimmed with red poppies. It would match the long red-silk gloves that were still in the bottom of my trunk.

Such a new little schoolhouse greeted us. There were two windows on each of three sides. The other side was taken up by the blackboard. Dora and I went all around it, marvelling at the shiny blackboard and the new window-glass. Dora counted the erasers and long sticks of chalk. The floor was shining yellow pine, and the door even had a lock on it. But the old scarred benches were the same.

"I had hoped there would be new ones," I told Dora.

"It takes so much money to build a new schoolhouse, there were none left for new benches and a teacher, too," she said. "We wanted you, Miss Prissy. We can sit on old benches."

The children came to school scrubbed and happy about their new schoolhouse. Several weeks went by without a trustee showing his face. The doctor had gone to Kentucky on some business and might not even get back while I was there. I tried not to show my disappointment at that.

One Friday late in April Dora and I took the short cut across the big pasture. Great patches of Indian paintbrush, sweeps of daisies and blue lupines, made the rolling prairie into an oversized patchwork quilt. Dora ran here and there, picking flowers. As I followed the path over a rise, I suddenly came face to face with a big red bull. Both of us too startled to move, we stared each other in the eye for a full minute. Then the bull took a step in my direction, whether out of curiosity or out of resentment I never knew. But I was sure his next move would bring a quick lunge with lowered horns and I would end up sailing through the air. I threw books and dinner bucket away.

"Dora," I screamed, "the bull—it's a bull," and charged back the way I had come. I had not gone ten steps when I landed practically in the arms of Preacher Higgins.

"What's hurtin' ye, Miss Prissy?" He held me by my shaking arms. "You hurt bad?"

"It's the bull—I mean that—he's chasing me."

The preacher pointed across the rise. There, on the far side of the gully, grazing peacefully, was the bull. Dora was picking flowers almost under his feet.

"That bull's not give' to chasin' folks," Preacher Higgins said. "He's my bull. I raised him gentle."

I tried to stop shaking. "I am afraid of cattle. They always chase me."

The preacher went for my books and dinner bucket. "I'll walk you acrost the pasture, Miss Prissy. You're not fitten to look after yourself, shakin' like that."

Dora followed, humming loudly, a dozen steps or so behind us. At the edge of the pasture Preacher Higgins pointed to a two-room log house with a corncrib and a shed beyond.

"That's my place," he said. "Forty acres of good bottom land, and not a dollar owin' on it. I've got a team of mules and that bunch of cows you jest passed. I'm fixed purty good, Miss Prissy."

"You certainly are, and I can see you are a good worker. Things look neat around your place."

"My wife's been dead six year. She was a good woman, but she's gone now. I need a woman, and I 'low you'd make a good wife. You could keep on teachin' the school. The money would come in handy."

He stood there, twisting a loop of rope as he talked, his thin face working with emotion.

I backed away. The ardent look in his eyes frightened me more than the bull did.

"Preacher Higgins, I'd never make a good wife for you. You should have one of those pretty girls around here who can hoe corn and milk your cows. I could never do that."

The preacher frowned. "You mean you won't marry me

account of the cows? I could sell them, or milk 'em myself."

"It's not entirely the cows, preacher. You see, I like some-one else."

For a minute I thought he would cry. His eyes filled like a hurt child's. Then without a word he turned and dis-appeared into the thicket. I waited for Dora to catch up with me.

"What happened, Miss Priss? I thought the preacher was going to walk you home." Dora's freckled face crinkled with mischievous laughter.

"He changed his mind, Dora. He found out I am afraid of cows."

On Saturday Page came home with big news. Dr. Ashton was back from Kentucky, and Page had invited him to Sunday dinner. The doctor sent word he would like to take Priss for a ride after dinner if she would go.

"You going, Prissy?" Hetty asked hopefully.

"We'd have to tie her in the bull pen to keep her here," Page said.

Hetty liked my new tan voile Mama had made for me. It had a low neck and short sleeves and was trimmed with tiny red buttons. I had slept with my hair in curlers and pinned it back as Dozie had done the day of the parade.

"Prissy, you have sure done it this time," Hetty said admiringly.

"Done what, Hetty?"

"You have made a lady of yourself for sure. Nobody would ever guess you once wore Punk Willard's pants."

The doctor looked me over, smiling as he held my hand. "What a pretty young lady and always the height of fash-ion. I am afraid Oak Grove can't keep you long, Priss. I am glad that young man can't see you now, or he would never let you stay."

After dinner, while Page and the doctor went to harness

the team, I put on my fancy new hat with the red-chiffon ties. For the first time I pulled on the long red-silk gloves that Mama had given me.

"I never thought I would wear them," I said, laughing.

"Well, if you don't catch the doctor in that outfit, you never will," Hetty said, teasing me. "It's the best yet."

"You make me feel like one of these man-chasing women, Hetty." I made a face at her.

Hetty grunted. "Well, that's about the size of it, young lady."

The drive was pleasant. The team stepped out like real harness racers. It was exciting to watch them go, and the doctor handled the reins expertly. His hands looked as if they had never held an ax or a saw nor guided a plow. He talked of his visit home to Kentucky.

"It's a fine country, Prissy, with pretty women, fine horses, and old whiskey. I would like to show it to you some-time."

For miles we drove over the prairie road. The thin veil of clouds along the western horizon turned to rose and then to gray. In another hour it would be dark—in another hour we would be back at the Carters'.

Dr. Ashton stopped the horses. "I have to open the gate. Do you think you can drive through, or had I better do it?"

"Of course I can drive through," I replied indignantly. Then I remembered I must be a lady. "At least, I think I can," I added demurely.

"Well, go ahead," he said doubtfully as he got down to open the gate, "but easy on the reins. These horses are bred to run."

Nettled, I gave the bays a smart slap with the reins. Instantly they were off, the light buggy no more than a trainer's cart behind them. Papa's buckskins could run, but these horses were like the speed of light. Thrilled and excited, I was having the time of my life. At last I was driving real horses, bred to run, with miles of open prairie before me.

Papa would be proud of me now if he could see me handling a pair of harness racers. Suddenly I remembered the poor doctor on the road behind us. I tried to slow the horses so I could turn around. It was then that I realized they were running away, and I did not have Papa beside me to take over. "Horses and men—" he had said. "Give them a light rein, but hold them steady."

That was a long time ago. With silk gloves I could not do much about holding them steady. The reins slipped through my silk gloves as if greased. If I could get the gloves off—but that was impossible. I could not do anything but try to hold the running horses. Papa had said to circle them and let them get their run out. Somehow I managed to wrap the reins around my hands, and they held. Steadily I circled the team and finally got them back on the road.

Far ahead I saw the doctor running toward me, but before we reached him, I had the bays pulled down to a walk, their flanks black with sweat and their nostrils quivering. I was weak with relief, realizing what might have happened.

"Thank God you're safe, Priscilla. I should never have let you handle that team. If anything had happened to you—"

I handed over the reins. I peeled off the red-silk gloves and tossed them with my hat onto the seat. "Never again will I be caught with those things on."

"What's wrong, Prissy? You look lovely today, and you certainly can handle horses. For a lady, you are the best I have ever seen."

"What's wrong?" I repeated. "Everything. I might have been killed or crippled because of those silly gloves. And I wore them just to make an impression on you. That's why. I wanted you to think I am a lady, but I am not. I can ride, and I can drive horses when I use my head, but I am no lady, and I don't want to be." My hair was down and my hands, without the gloves, might have been a boy's. "I tried, first for Mama's sake, and then for yours, to be a real lady. I—I even chased you. Hetty said so."

"Let me tie up the horses," the doctor said. "I must talk to you, child."

So I was a child again. But it didn't matter now.

"Now, Priss, let me help you out." He took my hand.

"But I am not a child. I am a grown woman," I said, flaring. "Can't you see that yet? Are you blind?"

He held both my hands in his. "You are a child and a woman, Prissy. I have loved you for it since that day I saw you on the fence—Sonny."

"Then you knew I was Sonny?"

"Of course." He was still breathless from his run. His hair lay wet against his head, but his eyes were laughing. Why, he was fun. I was not afraid of him, and I didn't need to worry about impressing him.

"Silly girl. I liked you as Sonny, and I like you as a dressed-up lady, but most of all I like the sweet young girl you are."

I turned away, embarrassed.

"Wait, Prissy. I want to ask you something. Are you engaged to Rick?"

"No, but he asked me to wait."

"Prissy, I could ask you to marry me. I could take you to Kentucky to live, and I would try to make you happy. But you don't really love me. I have tried to make myself think so, but I know better." His eyes were sad for a moment, then lighted with a smile. "But you weren't chasing me, Prissy. I encouraged you because I wanted to believe you were for me."

Suddenly I felt much older. "I think we had better go," I said.

He dropped my hands. "Is it Rick?"

"Yes, but I didn't know until now. I thought it was you."

The doctor sighed. "You were such an adorable tomboy, but you have grown up, and I am afraid you will never be Sonny again. I envy Rick."

When I went into the house, Page and Hetty were waiting supper for me.

"I thought the doctor would come in. I asked him," Hetty said.

"No, he drove off when I got out," I answered.

Hetty smiled at me. "It's Rick, after all, isn't it?"

I nodded.

The end of my three months finally came, and at last I was home again. Papa let me out at the back and went on to put up the team. As I walked along the orchard path to the house I thought I had never seen the place so beautiful. Mama and Rick were picking early cherries from the big tree near the house.

Rick dropped his bucket when he saw me.

"Prissy," he called, running toward me. He caught me in his arms and swung me up and then brought me down, as in the Cherry Dance, and kissed me. "Prissy, Prissy," he said, happier than I had ever seen him. "I got your letter, but let me hear you say the words. I want to hear you say you love me."

"Yes, Rick," I said, "I love you; I do, I do, but put me down."

"And you are not going back," he said, persisting.

"No, this is the end of the 'new-cut road.'"

Rick smiled and shook his head. "Not the end—only another turning. The road goes on and on, but from here the two of us will travel it together."

Just then Pinky came running up. "Hey, Priss, y'wanta see the filly? She's in the lot."

I tweaked his ear. "Not now, Pinky. The filly can wait."

Hand in hand, Rick and I went on to where Mama was busily picking cherries.